Praise for Alison Stone's
Random Acts

"This romance with a slightly inspirational flavor is recommended for readers who are looking for a sweet, 'clean' romance that still packs an emotional punch."

~ *Library Journal*

"Built with elements of suspense, emotion, a little bit of inspiration, and characters that are well worth reading about, Ms. Stone creates a heartwarming and intriguing tale in *Random Acts*. The pacing flows great, there's not a moment that's dull and I was left guessing until the very end."

~ *Sizzling Hot Book Reviews*

"I love it when a story grabs me in the first paragraph and puts me right there IN the story."

~ *Guilty Pleasures Book Reviews*

Look for these titles by
Alison Stone

Now Available:

Random Acts
Too Close to Home

Random Acts

Alison Stone

SAMHAIN
PUBLISHING

Samhain Publishing, Ltd.
11821 Mason Montgomery Road, 4B
Cincinnati, OH 45249
www.samhainpublishing.com

Random Acts
Copyright © 2013 by Alison Stone
Print ISBN: 978-1-60928-938-6
Digital ISBN: 978-1-60928-824-2

Editing by Heidi Moore
Cover by Kendra Egert

First Samhain Publishing, Ltd. electronic publication: April 2012
First Samhain Publishing, Ltd. print publication: March 2013

Dedication

To my husband, Scott, who never lost faith in me. Love you forever and always.

Chapter One

The Protector yanked open the back door of the girl's beat-up car. The door groaned in protest, the loud sound splintering the stagnant night air. He pulled at his collar, cursing the heat. October nights usually meant fleece jackets and first frosts, not suffocating mugginess. He swiped the back of his hand across his forehead but didn't stop. He had to work fast.

The dome light stood out like a beacon, making his pulse spike. He reached in and punched the plastic cover, casting them once again in darkness. A twig snapped behind him. He jerked to a stop and listened. Hard. The tiny hairs on the back of his neck prickled to life and a bead of sweat rolled down his back. As if in slow motion, he turned on his heel, the loose gravel shifting under his weight. Complete darkness. A chorus of crickets and night critters, but nothing else.

He drew in a deep breath and forced his attention back to the vehicle. The girl lay unconscious. Her head lolled at an awkward angle over the edge of the narrow back seat. A trickle of blood snaked out from one of her nostrils, her delicate lips swollen. His stomach clenched and he cursed under his breath. Tamping down the swirl of emotions, he crouched down into the vehicle and jammed his hands under her armpits. And pulled.

She was heavy, man, she was heavy, but it was dead weight. Or almost-dead weight. He brushed the sweat from his forehead on the top of his sleeve again. As her body cleared the vehicle, her bare feet thudded onto the gravel.

Frowning, he laid her body on the cool earth. With one knee on the back seat, he angled his body to search the vehicle, straining to see despite the inky darkness he had created. He patted the floor under the driver's seat, then under the others. No shoes. Where were her shoes?

Sheer fright swept over him. Even the night creatures seemed to whisper their disapproval. How could he have been so stupid? No one would believe she had gone out in the middle of the night without shoes.

He spun around and crouched back down by the girl. The fear in his gut morphed into anger. Fury. Why did it have to end this way? Resting an elbow on his knee, he trailed a finger along her nose, feeling the ridge of broken bone beneath his touch. Ah, such a pretty one. But not worth the aggravation. They never were.

Leaning closer, he held a hand under her nose. A whisper of air danced across his fingers. Sitting back on his heels, he pressed his lips together and shook his head. Man, she was a fighter. He had to admire that. But alive, she was a liability.

The moon poked out between drifting clouds. The girl's pale skin took on an ethereal glow. Her peaceful expression contradicted the abnormal angle of her broken nose and the bruises blooming underneath her dark lashes. A cold puff of apprehension dotted his damp flesh with goose bumps. Could he do it? Could he finish the job?

You are a man. A stern voice barked in his brain. *You do what is necessary.*

The gravel bit into his knee through the fabric of his pants as he got into position to lift her body, one arm under her armpits, the other under her knees. With a groan, he rose to his feet and cradled her body close to his. Too close. The clean scent of her damp hair tickled his nostrils. He didn't want to make this personal. A certain distance made his task easier to carry out.

Eager to be done with her, he kicked the back door shut with his boot. The rusty hinges and sound of metal meeting metal made him curse.

He was off his game tonight. It had been a long time. He bobbled her body, freeing his hand to grab the handle of the driver's door. It opened with a groan. He loosened his jaw and let out a quiet breath. A dog barked in the not-too-far distance. An incessant bark, as if the animal sensed the girl's plight.

His stomach tightened. His actions took on a renewed urgency. Swallowing hard, he maneuvered the girl's body behind the wheel—no small feat, despite her small frame. Her lifeless body had a will of its own. Her head dipped toward the passenger's side, physics demanding her body follow suit. His jaw clamped in frustration. He grabbed her shirt sleeve and yanked her back into position. With a flat palm, he pushed the door closed, careful not to make a sound this time. He reached through the open window to adjust her body one last time. Fastening her seatbelt would be counterproductive. He shook his head. Silly girl had only herself to blame. Ducking his head, he reached into the vehicle and stretched across the steering wheel to put the car in neutral.

With his plan coming together, he relaxed his shoulders and strolled to the rear of the vehicle. Some things were meant to be savored. He lifted a dusty boot to the plastic bumper.

And pushed.

The tires gained traction. The vehicle rolled forward. Arms crossed, he watched the vehicle pick up speed as it raced down the steep hill, heading toward the crop of trees at the bend in the road.

Just as he had planned.

Danielle Carson drew her knuckles tenderly across her sister's bruised cheek. Jenny didn't open her eyes. Didn't flinch. The constant, subtle *beep, beep, beep* of a monitor hammered away at her nerves, already jacked up on too much caffeine, no sleep and a red-eye flight from Atlanta to Buffalo, the first available after she had learned of her sister's car accident.

Icy dread coursed through Danielle's veins as she took in her sister's frail body under the white hospital linens. Her bandaged nose, darkened eyes and swollen lips made her almost unrecognizable. A fist of fear tightened around her heart as her gaze fell on the dried blood by her baby sister's hairline.

She let out a shaky breath. *Critical, but stable.* That's what the nurse had told her when she'd arrived at the hospital. Not at all what *he* had told her during that dreadful early-morning phone call.

She leaned over and pressed a kiss to Jenny's temple. The familiar scent of shampoo—the same cheap strawberry kind they had used as kids—tickled her nose. Tears blurred her vision as memories of her little sister crowded in on her.

"Oh, Jenny," she whispered, a question in her lament. "What happened?" Danielle wished her sister's bright, blue eyes would snap open and she'd reply with some witty comeback like, "I played chicken with a tree, and the tree won."

A creak sounded behind Danielle so she swiped a hand across her wet cheek. She bit her lower lip to keep it from trembling, even though she knew the nurse would understand. Drawing in a breath, she turned on her heel and her heart stopped. Instead of finding a nurse in scrubs, she found Officer

Patrick Kingsley standing in the doorway, dressed in a white uniform shirt and black pants, hat in hand, a solemn expression on his face.

"Glad you made it." He tossed his hat on the seat near the end of the bed and took a step toward her. Her body stiffened at his proximity.

"She's my sister." Her traitorous heart fluttered. She hadn't seen Patrick in fifteen years. Hadn't heard his voice until a few hours ago when he had called with news of the accident. In her hazy state of mind, it had taken her a few moments to understand why the person who had crushed her teenage heart all those years ago was calling in the middle of the night. What she had thought was a warped dream had quickly become a real-life nightmare.

"Any change?" Patrick seemed to be studying her face. She was sure her neck and cheeks were beet red by now. Was he, like her, amazed how time had a way of transforming a person's features? He appeared the same, yet different somehow. As if not only time but life's journey had subtly changed nuances of his features. The room suddenly felt smaller. A warmth flowed through her body. Maybe he wouldn't notice the pulse leaping in her neck.

"No. No change in Jenny's condition." Danielle's words came out strained. Being in his presence reminded her of the insecure teen she had once been. The one who had been abandoned by her mother, yet still had clung to the magical idea of happily-ever-after. Patrick had made her believe. Until he'd left her too.

The sting of that summer had the potential to slice her heart, even now. Unable to raise her eyes to meet his, Danielle shifted her attention back to Jenny. She was deeply angry with herself for even thinking about Patrick while her sister lay broken and battered.

"She's a mess. Why didn't you tell me on the phone? You made it seem like she was okay." Danielle despised the tremble in her voice.

When the silence stretched for too long, she persisted, "Why weren't you upfront with me? You should have told me—" she lowered her voice out of respect for Jenny, "—the truth about her condition." She stroked her thumb across her sister's hand, careful to avoid the bandage covering the tubes inserted into her veins. Her stomach did a little flip. There was a reason she had studied law instead of medicine, despite her grandmother's wishes.

"You had to fly from Atlanta alone," Patrick said— a statement, not a question.

Alone? She bristled. Why had Patrick Kingsley assumed she had to travel alone? Her grandmother had probably filled him in. Had told him how she spent all her time working and didn't have time for anything or anyone else. She berated herself for feeling even the slightest bit embarrassed. Hadn't she created the life she wanted? Being alone wasn't a sin. Relieved she didn't have to meet his gaze, she covered her sister's hand with her own. Why did she care what he thought?

"Would you have changed your plans if you knew the seriousness of her condition?" His voice grew closer. Still refusing to turn around, she sensed him standing a foot or two off her right shoulder. He was much broader than she remembered. Of course he was. The person she knew had been a boy. Standing here was a man. A man who had gotten married, been deployed to Iraq and experienced the tragedy of losing his wife. A tragedy beyond anything she had ever known.

"Tell me what you know about my sister's accident," Danielle said. She braced for the answer, needing to ground herself in the moment. In the details. Like how her sister's jagged nails stood in contrast to her own manicured pink tips. Gently, she turned over her sister's hand. Calluses toughened Jenny's fingertips, no doubt from hours working in the flower shop.

Endless questions swirled in her brain. How had her sister ended up in a one-vehicle accident down some lonely road? Had she been on her way to visit someone? Had she been drinking? She mentally shook her head. No way. She refused to believe that. Not after everything their alcoholic mother had put them through as kids.

The sharp edge of fear poked at her. *How would you know? You haven't been home in over a year. Closer to two.* She pushed the thought aside and searched for more logical reasons. Texting maybe? An animal darting into the road? Millions of valid reasons didn't include alcohol.

But she needed to know. Uncertainty and unanswered questions made her skin crawl. Maybe if she controlled a little bit of what was going on, the knot in her stomach would ease.

Patrick hesitated. She sensed he was holding back, measuring his words. She refused to be spoon-fed. "Tell me, Patrick. I'm a big girl. I can handle whatever it is you have to say. Was she drinking?" She folded the edge of the sheet and smoothed it between her fingers, her pulse roaring in her ears.

"I don't have much to tell." Tendrils of unease wound their way up her spine as he spoke. "We're waiting on the toxicology reports, but at this time we don't believe she was drinking." He touched her shoulder, his solid hand warm and comforting.

All part of his job, she quickly reminded herself.

"A passerby noticed her car off the road on Route 78 about one in the morning," he added.

"Where was she going?" She glanced over her shoulder and

his fingers brushed her cheek.

"We're still investigating."

Danielle shook her head and backed away from his touch. She needed to think. She dug her fingers under her hair at the back of her neck. A tension headache spread up the base of her brain. "Please, tell me whatever it is you know." The Patrick she had known always had such an open, honest face, but now his expression seemed shuttered. Her stomach clenched. Was he hiding something from her? Or had age taught him how to hide his feelings?

Running a hand across his chin, Patrick's gaze shifted to Jenny. Reluctance was evident in his eyes. "We found Jenny's vehicle off the road. Wedged between two trees. She was unconscious." Fully meeting her gaze, his eyes darkened. His broad chest expanded with a deep breath before he let it out slowly. "No skid marks. No witnesses. No other victims."

A realization crept into her consciousness. Jenny's frail condition pained Patrick. Why hadn't she noticed right away? Mayport was a small town. Everyone knew each other, and Patrick lived next door to Jenny and her grandmother. He knew Jenny. Probably better than she did.

"I'm sorry." She pressed her palm to her forehead and blinked back the tears. She turned around, unwilling to break down in front of him. She reached over and ran a strand of Jenny's soft auburn hair—the same shade as her own—through her fingers. "I'm trying to make sense of it."

He cupped her shoulder, sending a warm tingle across her flesh. She resisted the urge to lean into him for comfort.

"Sometimes these things don't make sense. We have to trust in God's plan," he said in a soothing voice.

Danielle lowered her head and gritted her teeth. Trust didn't come easily to her.

16

"Would you like to say a prayer?"

Danielle's mouth worked, but the words wouldn't come. A flush of goose bumps blanketed her skin. She tilted her head. The heat from Patrick's hand radiated up to her cheek. She had long ago given up on prayer and on God. Yet, something subtle chipped away at the armor surrounding her heart. Who was she to deny her sister the benefit of a prayer? Even if in her heart of hearts she didn't believe it would work.

"Okay," she whispered through a too-tight throat. Her acquiescence stemmed more from superstition—or maybe feelings of helplessness—than fear of God.

"Heavenly Father—" Patrick bowed his head, one hand still on Danielle's shoulder, the other rested on Jenny's forearm, "—please place Your hands upon Jenny. Guide the doctors and nurses responsible for her care. Heal her body. Watch over her and protect her. We lay this in Your hands. Amen."

Patrick kept his head bowed in prayerful silence. She tried to do the same, but the beeping monitor invaded her peaceful thoughts. His comforting touch now seemed too intimate. Too close. Too much weight on her thin shoulder.

Danielle ducked away from him and snatched her overnight bag from the floor near the foot of the bed. Working her lower lip, she hoisted the strap of the bag over her shoulder. "I need to see Gram. Make sure she's okay. The nurse said the physician wouldn't be available to meet until later this afternoon. I may as well go now." The words spilled out as Danielle tried to make sense of the earth shifting under her feet.

In order to restore order, she needed to do something concrete. Create a list. Check things off. Because standing over her sister's broken body saying prayers to a God who had long ago forsaken her, brought her back to a dark place she didn't care to revisit.

"I'll take you home to Gram," Patrick said, concern softening his rugged features.

An unexpected smile tugged at the corner of Danielle's mouth. She had forgotten the familiar way in which he referred to her grandmother. Although Gram had never come out and said it, Danielle suspected she'd always had a special place in her heart for Patrick—the kind teen who had taken her grandchildren under his wing even though his own mother had given him grief for it.

"Come on." Patrick reached for her overnight bag. She let the strap drop from her shoulder. Handing the bag over to him, their fingers brushed. A warm tingle surged up her arm, threatening to undo all the years she had worked to forget about the boy next door. To forget the fantasy of a silly teenager.

Patrick had run off and married someone else, hadn't he? That fact had always sobered her up quickly.

He held out his palm, inviting her to walk ahead of him. She lifted her index finger and returned to her sister's side. She pressed a gentle kiss to Jenny's warm forehead. "Rest well, baby sis." Tears pricked the back of her eyes.

"She's going to be okay." Patrick's voice sounded husky behind her.

Danielle's eyes slid shut and she nodded, unable to speak around a lump of emotion. Faith gave people hope. She wished a person could learn faith from a textbook. She had always been a good student. But some things just were. Or, in her case, weren't.

She leaned in close so only her sister could hear. "Please be okay. You can't leave me and Gram."

When she turned around, she found Patrick studying her with kind eyes. Heat swept up her neck and warmed her cheeks. Had he heard her childish plea? Inwardly, she shook her head. No one heard her whisper.

Not even Patrick's God.

Chapter Two

"You're not going to make me sit in the back, are you?" Danielle shot Patrick a sideways glance as they approached his police cruiser, a hint of mischief sparking in her blue eyes. A wry smile graced her pink lips. A brisk wind gusted across the hospital parking lot and she tugged her jacket closed. She seemed a lot more sophisticated and thinner than he remembered, but she still had the same quick wit.

He opened the front passenger's door. "Promise me you won't play with the siren."

She arched a brow. "No promises."

Once they were both settled in the car, he turned the key in the ignition. "Did you want to stop for lunch before we go to Gram's? You've been on the road a long time."

"No. Thanks," she added, if by way of afterthought. "I'm anxious to see Gram. She must be beside herself." Without waiting for an answer, she pulled out her cell phone and checked the display. She let out a long sigh through tight lips. "I wish I could leave the office for one day without—" she raised her phone, "—this."

"Indispensable, huh?" He suspected she didn't take many days off. The way Gram talked, it sounded like she rarely left the office.

She pressed a few buttons on one of those fancy touch-screen cell phones. "I'd like to think so." A mirthless smile touched her pink lips. "But haven't you heard? Lawyers are a dime a dozen." A thin line creased her forehead. "If I walked out the door today, there would be twenty lawyers lined up for my job in the morning." She shook her head. "There's no such thing as job security anymore."

He opened his mouth to say something but her finger shot up in a hold-on-a-minute gesture. She lifted the phone to her ear.

Danielle was still fiddling with her cell phone when they arrived at Gram's house. From what he'd gathered, she had a lot of projects at work in need of attention, and nothing short of an emergency would have drawn her back to Mayport.

He had a hard time believing it had been less than twelve hours since he had dialed Danielle's number and heard her sleepy voice across the line. Her sweet voice, much like an old song, had immediately taken him back. Nostalgia and longing had flooded a part of his heart he thought had died with his wife. *What if?* What if things had been different back then? What if this was their second chance? He mentally shook his head. *You're tired. You're on edge from last night.* He refused to give credence to anything he was feeling right now. Besides, he had someone more important in his life now.

As he eased the cruiser up the rutted driveway, the car rocked back and forth. For the first time since they had left the hospital, his passenger's head snapped up. An annoyed expression marred the delicate features of her narrow face. She planted her free hand on the dashboard for balance. "The driveway's a mess."

"The snowplow guy did a number on it last winter."

"This place is getting too much for Gram to maintain." Danielle ran her finger along her chin. He followed her gaze to the white farmhouse at the top of the drive and tried to see it through her eyes—crumbling roof tiles, dingy siding and unkempt landscaping.

"Maybe I should encourage her to put the house on the market. Downsize. Get some money for the house while she can."

"Don't tell my mother," Patrick said dryly.

"Bunny's still selling real estate?" Tilting her head, Danielle cut him a sideways look "She'd have the For Sale sign planted in the yard by sundown. And knowing your mother—" an unexpected flicker of amusement danced in her eyes, "—she's probably already drafted a copy of the real-estate listing." She tapped her lips with the edge of her cell phone and stared off in the distance. "Let's see. Park-like setting. Real charmer. Needs TLC. Must see inside. Oh—" she lifted a finger, "—and great neighbors."

He touched a finger to his nose and pointed at her. "You nailed it. You couldn't ask for better neighbors than yours truly." He patted her hand and was rewarded with a genuine smile. "I think you missed your calling," he said in a light teasing tone before getting out of the car.

Danielle climbed out her side and slammed the door. "I really appreciate the ride." She turned and twisted her ankle in a deep rut. He grabbed her forearm to steady her.

"You okay?"

"Fine." Red crept up her neck. He remembered how easily she blushed. "These silly shoes." She glanced down at the high heels poking out from underneath her jeans. "You'd think I would have grabbed tennis shoes on my way out the door this morning."

Patrick shrugged. A nonanswer. But tennis shoes did seem more practical than high-heeled boots. Somehow he guessed

Danielle was more about fashion than practicality. She certainly presented herself as put together. Totally professional. *Attractive*. Yet, the rough-and-tumble Danielle, the freshman girl who had moved in next door when he was a senior in high school, had been the one to catch his eye. Not that he didn't enjoy the updated version.

He closed his eyes briefly. There he went again, pining for the old days. He yanked open the back door of his cruiser and grabbed her bag. "I'll take this in for you." He hiked the bag's strap up onto his shoulder.

"Please, you've done enough. I'm sure you have to get back to work."

"I am working."

Danielle's shoulders seemed to drop a fraction. "I know...I mean, I'm sure you have other work to do."

"Listen, I know it's hard for you to be back here."

Her eyes widened, then immediately narrowed. "My job keeps me busy in Atlanta." Her words framed a challenge.

"It's more than that, isn't it?" He tilted his head, trying to catch her averted gaze. "You didn't have the easiest childhood here."

"A very astute observation, Officer Kingsley. Are you a psychologist now or just a fan of Dr. Phil?"

Patrick stifled a small chuckle. "Dr. Phil, huh? Listen, I didn't mean to..." His words trailed off.

"I really do appreciate your being here for Gram... even though it is *your job*." She put undue weight on the last two words. "But I'm okay." She reached for the bag. "Really, I can carry my own bag. I'm not some helpless damsel in distress." She batted her long eyelashes for emphasis.

He twisted his lips, studying her. "Suit yourself." He pulled the strap off his shoulder and held out the bag. When he released the strap, her hand dropped with the weight of it.

She put the strap over her shoulder and suddenly seemed impatient. "I'll see you later."

"If it's all the same to you," Patrick said, "I'll collect my daughter." Her eyes widened in surprise. He tipped his head toward the house. "Come on, I'll get the door for you."

The gravel crunched under Danielle's feet. "I didn't think Gram would be up for babysitting." A hint of irritation threaded her tone. Apparently sensing it, she lifted a hand, a look of contrition settling on her pretty features. "I didn't mean to snap. I'm just tired."

"I understand." He turned the handle and pushed on the door with his shoulder. One of these days he was going to fix the side door for Gram. It had swelled in its frame, making it difficult to open and close. "But I wouldn't exactly call it babysitting," Patrick said, holding the door open for her. "It's more like keeping each other company."

Danielle followed Patrick into the house. He disappeared into the family room while she drew up short in the kitchen. The familiar smell, a musty mix of Lemon Pledge and stale air, always made her breath hitch in her lungs. Gram sealed up the house tight at the first threat of frost. "No sense heating the outside," she'd say.

The smell never failed to evoke the powerful memory of her first visit. Exhaling slowly, Danielle tried to calm her nerves. The familiar tingling had already started in her fingertips. Distracting herself, she soaked in the details of the room. The orange, stained linoleum and matching counters were a testament to the flower-powered seventies, dated even when she'd first laid eyes on them. All this was in stark contrast to the builder upgrades she had chosen prior to moving into her high-end townhouse in Atlanta.

Danielle tossed her overnight bag onto the chair. Hard to believe she was once a frightened fourteen-year-old girl whose mother had unceremoniously dumped off her and her sister to run away with the boyfriend *du jour*. At the time, Danielle had carried a white kitchen-garbage bag with all their belongings, the thin plastic stretching under her grip. Her baby sister had clutched a Superstar Barbie dressed in a fashionable pink gown with matching boa. Thinking about the doll made Danielle's heart ache. At ten, when most girls were tiring of dolls, Jenny had clung tightly to her only prized possession.

"Are you going to come in?" Patrick's question snapped her out of her reverie. Without waiting for an answer, he grabbed an apple from the fruit bowl on the counter and took a big bite. He swiped the back of his hand across his mouth and a hint of a smile lit his green eyes. When he returned to the living room, she closed her eyes, savoring the secret thrill zinging through her body. *Man, he's handsome.*

"Should I challenge you?" Gram's frail voice drifted in from the family room. She sounded exhausted.

"No, I promise it's a real word," a little girl said. *Patrick's daughter.* Heat washed over her. Her mind raced. She hadn't even asked his daughter's name. *Great.*

Danielle moved toward the archway separating the kitchen and living room. She hung back unnoticed, watching the father-daughter exchange. Her heart swelled with an emotion that caught her off guard. Patrick rested his hand affectionately on his daughter's shoulder. In her mind, Danielle had envisioned his child to be younger, preschool aged maybe. But the girl playing Scrabble with Gram was not yet a teen, but close. She hadn't been around enough kids to know her exact age. But one thing she did know. His daughter was beautiful. Long, wavy blonde hair like her late mother's.

A sharp, sudden pain stabbed her heart. A personal pain. An overwhelming desire to draw this child into an embrace—to tell her she understood what it was like to grow up without a mother—swept over her.

"I don't know, Gram. Do you think Ava's trying to fake you out?" Father and daughter leaned over the Scrabble board. Gram tipped her head back and glanced down, trying to see through her bifocals.

Ava playfully swatted Patrick's hand and shifted in her seat, jutting out her lower lip. *"Dad..."* She rolled her eyes, then suddenly froze. Her back stiffened.

Patrick followed his daughter's gaze, his green eyes landing on Danielle. Her cheeks grew warm. Again. Why did this man, even after all these years, have such a strong effect on her?

Danielle pushed off the arched doorway and forced a smile past the uneasiness swirling in her belly. "Hello." She crossed to Gram and pressed a kiss to her soft cheek. The sweet scent of butterscotch tickled her nose. "How are you?"

Gram caught Danielle's hands and squeezed. Her blue eyes shimmered with unshed tears. "You came."

"Of course," Danielle said, her tone edged with indignation as she pulled her hands free. She lifted her eyes, mortified to find Patrick studying her. Averting her gaze, she struggled to shake off the guilt Gram's words had inflicted.

She tried again, this time softening her tone. "I went to the hospital first. Jenny's hanging in there. Would you like to go see her this afternoon?"

"That would be nice, dear." Gram twisted her hands in her lap. "I couldn't bear to see her earlier. But now you're here." The older woman bowed her head. "Thank God."

Danielle placed her hand over Gram's. "It'll be okay." The image of Jenny's battered face flitted across her brain. The words tasted like a lie on her lips.

Danielle turned around, but before she had a chance to introduce herself, Patrick placed a hand on his daughter's shoulder. "Ava, this is Miss Danielle." He lifted his other palm toward Danielle.

Ava's eyes sparkled with surprise. "Gram talks about you. You're the lawyer."

"I am." Unsure of the protocol with the preteen set, Danielle extended her hand. Ava took it hesitantly then quickly dropped her hand to her side.

"I've been praying for Miss Jenny," Ava said in a hushed tone.

Danielle wasn't sure what to say, but settled on a simple, "Thank you."

"How come I haven't met you before?" The innocence of Ava's question cut Danielle to the core.

"I live pretty far away." Danielle's simple answer did nothing—in her mind—to excuse the inexcusable. But how could a child understand the reasons she had avoided Mayport? Reasons even she struggled to understand.

"But you flew here today?" Ava's green eyes, the color and shape marking her as her father's daughter, twinkled. "I flew all the way over the ocean when we came back from the military base." She tilted her head and pressed her lips together as if giving it great thought. "But Atlanta is in Georgia, right? It's not *that* far."

Danielle wilted under the intensity of the girl's interrogation. "You're right. It's not. I guess work has kept me busy." Danielle crossed to the loveseat on the opposite wall and sat. Her fingers absentmindedly traced the delicate detail of the

27

crocheted doily on the arm of the furniture.

"My dad works a lot too," Ava said with the resigned authority of a child older than her years. "But—" her voice brightened, "—he gets to tuck me in every night, no matter what." The girl flashed a big smile at her dad.

Standing behind his daughter, Patrick gave her shoulders a playful squeeze. "Sometimes she's asleep when I get home, but I still get to kiss her goodnight." His deep love for his daughter rolled off him in waves.

"I'm never asleep when you come in. I wait up for you." Ava tipped her head back to look at him.

Patrick smiled and gently tugged a long strand of her hair. "I can hear you snoring."

"I never snore." Ava laughed. She shifted her focus to Danielle, her bright eyes sobering. "When I was little, Dad spent a long time in Iraq. Mom and I wouldn't see him for like forever."

"That had to be really hard." Danielle searched for the appropriate words. This charming little girl had suffered a lot of hurt in her short life, yet her eyes exhibited a spark, an energy that spoke volumes. Despite everything, she had a solid home. A father who loved her. And in the end—on the surface anyway—it seemed Ava wasn't the worse for wear.

"You're pretty good at Scrabble?" Danielle asked, changing the subject.

It was Ava's turn to lift a shoulder, then let it fall. She bowed her head and studied her shoes.

"She's being modest." Patrick nudged his daughter's shoulder. "She won the fifth-grade spelling bee."

Ava looked like she wanted to protest, but Gram lifted a shaky hand. "Learn how to take a compliment, child. God gave you a talent. With the proper schooling, you can do anything." Her eyes moved to Danielle. "Look at my granddaughter here, a big-time lawyer."

"The partners in the law firm might dispute that claim."

"Hey, sweetie," Patrick said to his daughter, "it's time to run home. Let your new friend get settled." He pressed a business card into Danielle's hand, the brief contact sending a delightful warm sensation up her arm. "Call me if you need anything." He paused and lifted an eyebrow. "Anything."

She ran her thumb across the embossed lettering of his name. "We'll be fine." Tucking the card into the back pocket of her jeans, she escorted Patrick and Ava out through the kitchen door.

When she returned to the living room, she found her grandmother with the Bible open in her lap. "Excuse me, Gram."

Her grandmother looked up expectantly.

"I'll make us some lunch before we go see Jenny."

"I'd like that." Gram placed her finger on the page to mark her spot.

Danielle spun on her heel, hoping to escape before Gram asked her to sit and read the Bible with her, something she had often done as a teen. If God was keeping track, she didn't want Him to call her out on her hypocrisy. Certainly not twice in one day.

"Dear..."

Danielle tossed a glance over her shoulder, fearing she was too late.

"Patrick's a good man," the older woman said.

"Yes, he is nice," she muttered and took another step toward the kitchen.

"He's a widower now. Tragic what happened to his wife." Gram pinned her with a gaze.

"Yes, it is."

"Sometimes God works in mysterious ways." Gram smoothed a hand across the Bible page, seemingly searching for the right words. "He's single. Maybe now..." She let the words trail off.

Danielle shook her head. "Gram, I'm here for Jenny. And for you. Nothing more." She took another step toward the kitchen. "Patrick is just doing his job."

"Dear, you wear your heart on your sleeve. Don't go passing up a perfectly good opportunity. Patrick has been a widower for two years now."

Danielle rolled her eyes, a smile pulling at her lips. Gram always told it like it was. "I'm not interested in Patrick," she said, not sounding very convincing.

Gram pursed her lips. "You need more in your life. All you do is work. Even the child saw that."

Danielle's eyes flared wide and she laughed. "You filled her head with that notion."

"But it's true."

Danielle waved her hand in dismissal. "Let me get your lunch."

Danielle strode into the kitchen and opened the fridge. The shelves were full. Jenny must have shopped recently. A pain squeezed her heart. How quickly life turned on a dime. One day you're grocery shopping and the next you're in a coma. Unease skittered down her spine. The recent events had driven her to distraction, making it impossible to do something as simple as pull together lunch.

Up until now, Danielle's adult life had been exactly the way she'd wanted it. She had a great job, a lot of responsibility, people who counted on her. With any luck, she'd make partner in twelve to eighteen months. Her plans didn't include starting a relationship. Her sole reason for returning to Mayport was for her family. For Jenny. Nothing more. Gram was old-fashioned. A woman didn't have to have a man to be complete.

"Danielle?" Gram called from the other room. "Are you standing with the fridge door open?"

Danielle grabbed the carton of eggs to make warm egg-salad sandwiches and closed the fridge door. Some things never changed.

Chapter Three

After lunch, Danielle escaped to the wide front porch, one of her favorite places. She loved the porch swing. But when it emitted a high-pitched creak, she quickly shifted her weight to the balls of her feet until she was satisfied the chains weren't going to rip from their anchors. Finally, she settled back and let the crisp autumn breeze caress her cheeks. The dried leaves scurried across the wooden porch, sending goose bumps across her flesh. She zipped the jacket she had borrowed from Jenny's closet, the fleece collar snug against her neck. Maybe the southern heat had thinned her blood.

Resigned she couldn't put it off any longer, she punched in her administrative assistant's number on her cell phone. The missed calls and voice-mail counters indicated Sandra had been trying to reach Danielle all morning. A nagging dread dogged her. She imagined impeccably groomed Sandra's distinct disapproval at being unable to reach Danielle. Sandra prided herself on efficiency and expected the same from the lawyers with whom she worked.

Danielle pressed the phone to her ear. "I've been trying to reach you," her assistant said, her frustrated tone not at all surprising. Sandra had started working for Danielle's boss some thirty years ago when the term *secretary* was still in vogue. When Danielle had been promoted last year, Sandra had suddenly added the youngest member of the firm to her slate of lawyers. She suspected Sandra wasn't very pleased but had taken on her newest charge with professionalism mixed with a moderate dose of stern mothering.

"What's going on?" Danielle was too tired to hide the edge in her tone. What could possibly have gone wrong at work already? She thought of the files stacked neatly on her desk. In reality, any number of problems might have cropped up. That's why she never took a day off.

"You left a brusque message regarding a family emergency?"

"My sister has been in a car accident." The reality of her words had yet to sink in.

"Oh dear," Sandra said, "I hope she's okay."

Me too. "Thank you." Danielle cleared her throat. "Is there something urgent at work?"

"Mr. McCoy had a few questions on the contract." McCoy was one of her biggest clients, a self-made millionaire real-estate developer. The kind of client her firm was known to represent. The kind who paid the bills.

"I'll get back to him." Danielle absentmindedly ran her hand along the rough edge of the wood swing.

"Never mind. I gave John the file."

"Oh..." She struggled to find the words. John was another young lawyer in the firm, one who'd love to home in on such a high-profile client. "Was that really necessary?"

"It couldn't wait." A sniff sounded across the line. "And Danielle?"

"Yes?" A flicker of apprehension washed over her.

"A Miss Tina Welch called." She said the words as if reading them from a note.

Danielle's heart dropped. *Tina Welch.* She was only supposed to call Danielle's cell phone. She slouched against the hard wood slats of the porch swing. Tina had probably left a voice mail. When Danielle hadn't gotten back to her sooner, Tina had probably become anxious and called the main switchboard. "Did she say what she wanted?" She tugged at the ponytail, freeing her hair. She pressed her fingers to the back of her neck, easing some of the pent-up frustration.

"No, but she sounded upset." Sandra paused. "I don't seem to have her name on file."

Tina usually was upset. Life hadn't dealt the young woman an easy hand. She was currently facing foreclosure and becoming homeless with her young son. Empathetic to her situation, Danielle had offered to help Tina on her own time. Sandra wouldn't understand. Neither would her bosses.

"It's personal." As soon as the words came out of Danielle's mouth, she wanted to call them back. Danielle didn't have a personal life. It's what made her excel at work. Gave her an edge when it came to promotions. The firm wouldn't be happy if they knew one of their lawyers wasted billable hours on a client who couldn't pay. Because technically all of her time was potentially billable hours.

"Did she leave a number?" Danielle tapped her fingers on the arm of the swing and shifted in her seat. Out of the corner of her eye, she noticed something moving. The tiny hairs on the back of her neck stood up. Snapping her head around, she pushed off the swing. She grabbed the chain to stop it from clattering against the railing. Narrowing her gaze, she scanned the dark edge of trees and bushes lining the property. A splash of orange caught her eye then vanished. Her pulse roared in her ears. The digits her assistant rattled off barely registered. It didn't matter. The number was undoubtedly on her list of missed calls.

"Okay, thanks." Distracted, Danielle ended the call. Wrapping her fingers around the sleek plastic of her cell phone, she pressed it to her chest. Was someone out there? Watching her?

The distinct sound of a twig snapping sent a surge of cold fear racing through her veins. Leaning on the wood railing, a white chip of paint dug into her palm. She cleared her throat. "Hello, is someone there?"

"Is everything okay?"

Danielle spun around, surprise and something akin to fear lighting her crystal-clear blue eyes. Patrick planted a foot on the bottom step of the porch and leaned on the railing with crossed arms. "*Is* everything okay?"

Danielle shook her head, her golden-auburn locks flowing freely over her shoulders. "I heard something over there." She pointed toward the trees. "Probably an animal."

"I'll check it out." He strolled toward the tree line and glanced over his shoulder at her. Something in Danielle's body language and intense gaze spoke of her genuine concern. He stepped carefully into the wooded area. A thick blanket of decaying leaves crunched under his feet. The tree branches above blocked the remaining light of the overcast afternoon, and a chill cut through the thin fabric of his uniform shirt as he scanned the deep shadows. He could barely make out the shapes of the trees, but nothing seemed out of the ordinary.

After listening in silence for a few moments, he returned to Danielle. "Must have been an animal. I've seen a few deer recently."

Briefly closing her eyes, she nodded. "I'm just jittery. Caffeine and lack of sleep. Not a good combination." She ran a hand through the loose strands of her hair.

"It's nice."

The corners of Danielle's delicate mouth turned down in confusion.

He jerked his chin toward her. "Your hair. It looks nice down."

She shrugged, seemingly self-conscious. "It's a mess."

Sensing he had said too much, Patrick lifted his hand, jangling a set of keys. "Left my vehicle in your driveway. Can't very well get back to work without it."

"Of course." She glanced at the police cruiser sitting in the driveway. "I'll have to rent a car. I hadn't expected to be in Mayport for more than a day or two."

"We can take care of that later. I'll bring you and Gram up to the hospital this afternoon."

"We've already taken too much of your time." She crossed to the top of the steps and tapped her fingers on the rail. "I'm sure you have *other* work to do."

"No rest for the weary."

"Right." The smile slipped from her face.

Had he said something to offend her?

Danielle pressed her lips together and bowed her head, seemingly studying the pile of leaves trapped at the bottom of the porch steps. After a beat of silence, she lifted her face, her expressive eyes radiating a deep hurt.

What was going on in her pretty little head? He mentally shook away the thought. *Never mind.* It was too easy to get emotionally caught up with Danielle considering their shared past.

"I'm sorry about your wife," Danielle said, her words jarring him. "I should have sent a card, but then too much time had passed..." The words trailed off and she looked down, her lashes sweeping her smooth cheeks.

"Thanks." He let out a long breath. "It's been a tough go."

"Gram told me you moved back last year." Lacing her fingers in front of her, she came down the porch steps, closing the distance between them, her soft floral fragrance awakening his senses.

"Ava and I tried to make a go of it on the base, but in the end we decided to move home. I needed Bunny's help." He stuffed his hands in his pockets and shrugged. "Not easy for a single dad to raise a daughter."

"I'm sure Bunny loves having her granddaughter to dote on."

Patrick laughed. "After raising two boys, she's in her glory. But you know Bunny. She loves Ava to pieces, but she refuses to be called Grandma. Kinda like how she never liked to be called Mom." He leaned back on the railing and let his eyes take in her delicate features. "It's great to see you." He reached out and brushed away a strand of hair caught on the corner of her mouth. He sensed a subtle flinch, but she didn't back away. "I wish it had been under different circumstances."

"Me too." Pink colored her cheeks.

"You haven't been home in a while."

"Work keeps me busy." A far-away look descended into her eyes. "And you were right earlier. It's more than that. This town doesn't exactly conjure up the best memories."

"I hope that doesn't include me."

She glared down her nose at him before a playful smile brightened her face. "I see your ego's intact."

"I never had a big ego." He furrowed his brow and jerked his head back in mock indignation.

Leaning in, her breath whispered across his cheek,

taunting him. "Give me a break. The hot-shot high school quarterback. Didn't you date the prom queen?"

Patrick ran a hand across his chin. "I wonder what happened to what's-her-name?"

She swatted at him. "I have a feeling you left a lot of girls in your wake." A serious expression darkened her eyes.

He dared to trace a finger down her smooth cheek, his eyes drifting to her soft, warm lips. Her features stilled. "You were so young," he said, his voice husky. "Had just graduated from high school. And my mother..." How could he put into words the confused emotions of a man barely out of his teens?

Shaking her head, Danielle took a few steps. The dead leaves crunched under her feet. "I'm glad you figured it out for the both of us."

He scrubbed a hand across his face. "Man, we *both* were young."

"You're right." She lifted her palms, her expression growing hard. "No harm. No foul. It was just a summer fling, right? You already had Lisa back at college."

"Lisa and I weren't dating that summer. I wouldn't have kissed you if I'd had a girlfriend." He reached out for her hand, but she stepped out of his grasp. "Is that what you thought?"

"Does it really matter?" She waved him away. "It was a lifetime ago."

It *did* seem like a lifetime ago. He and Danielle had been strictly friends for almost four years. Then he came home the summer after she graduated from high school and realized his tomboy neighbor had grown into a beautiful young woman. His heart tightened at the memory.

"I met Lisa the fall of my senior year in college," he explained. "We had one of those whirlwind romances. It made sense to get married when I graduated because I was being deployed."

Danielle nodded, her lips pressing into a thin line. A sheen of something he couldn't quite identify shone in her eyes.

"It *is* nice to see you." He reached out. This time he was able to squeeze her forearm. Had he sensed a quiet trembling?

"Nice to see you too." Danielle slipped past him. "It's chilly out here." She rubbed her hands down her arms. "I need to see if Gram is ready to go to the hospital." She disappeared into the house, leaving him standing in the cold.

Chapter Four

Danielle climbed into her childhood bed and pulled the covers to her chin, relieved to be alone. The trip to the hospital had left her exhausted and emotionally spent. Gram had nearly fainted when she had seen Jenny's bruised face and battered body. The fleeting nature of life was never more evident than when Danielle stood by her sister's hospital bed with her grandmother who suddenly seemed older than her years.

Danielle hated to admit it, but Patrick had been a huge comfort since this ordeal had begun. He had shown such warmth and compassion to both her and her grandmother. The familiar pangs of guilt twisted her insides. How had she moved away without a second thought, abandoning the only woman who had shown her love? The reality of the situation had become clear. Jenny needed her. Gram needed her.

But she had responsibilities in Atlanta.

Danielle flipped over her pillow and punched it. She curled up on her side and pressed her eyes closed. Sleep eluded her.

She wasn't sure how long she had been lying there dozing when suddenly she opened her eyes. Adrenaline surged through her veins. The blood in her ears roared, deafening her. Sucking in deep breaths, she struggled to shake the nauseating mix of panic and confusion. The obscure outlines in the darkened room were as disorienting as the jolt of emotions swirling through her system. Where was she? And what had startled her out of a fitful sleep?

Danielle pushed up on her elbow and blinked. The forms in the bedroom took shape. *Ah, my childhood bedroom.* The thick branches of the oak tree outside her window swayed in the wind, a few thin branches clacking against the exterior wall. The old windows rattled in their frames.

The large red letters on the digital clock read 3:33. Danielle lay back down and pulled the covers up, trying to get comfortable, but she feared she'd never get back to sleep, not with the events of the past twenty-four hours crowding in on her again.

She rubbed a hand across her eyes and tossed back the scratchy sheets. Why bother pretending? Her nerves were on overdrive. She swung her legs over the side of the bed and braced herself for the inevitable chill of the cold hard wood on her bare feet. Some things you never forgot. Her townhouse had plush carpeting in the bedroom.

She glanced toward the bathroom adjoining this room with her sister's. *Her sister...* "Jenny, where were you going? What made you run off the road?" Tears burned the back of her eyes. She took in a deep breath and exhaled slowly. Things always seemed much worse in the dark of night.

An idea struck her. One she should have considered earlier if her brain hadn't been frazzled. Between her sister's accident and seeing Patrick again, she hadn't thought of her sister's cell phone. Maybe there was a record of a phone call prior to her going out. She scratched her forehead. Did it really matter where Jenny was going? It wouldn't change the outcome. But it was just like her to try to put everything in a neat little box.

A crash sounded through the quiet air. She froze, still seated on the edge of the bed. Tiny pinpricks swept across her scalp. The strumming of her pulse in her ears made it impossible to hear. A thud vibrated the cold floor beneath her feet. Swallowing hard, she felt for her cell phone on the nightstand. Her clumsy movements knocked it to the wood floor with a resounding clatter. She sucked in a breath and glanced toward the door. Only shadows. And silence.

She got down on all fours and breathed a sigh of relief when her fingers brushed the hard plastic of her cell phone. After getting to her feet, she tiptoed across the frigid floor to the bathroom. Holding her breath, she paused in the doorway, straining to hear.

Another creak pierced the dead of night. Footsteps in the kitchen? She doubted Gram would venture downstairs at this hour. Panic seized her heart. No, Gram definitely wouldn't be wandering around the kitchen. She had helped her grandmother climb the stairs to her second-floor bedroom before retiring and it wasn't likely she'd wandered downstairs in the dark.

Heart racing, Danielle stepped back into the bathroom. She pulled the pocket door closed, cringing as the wheels scraped in their track. She slid the flimsy lock into place and raced to the adjoining door. She pulled on the handle, but it wouldn't budge. The door was stuck in the pocket, hung up on something in the track. Her mouth dry, she crossed her sister's darkened room, tripping on a pair of discarded shoes. Instinctively, she folded in pain, biting back a yelp. When did her sister get this messy? She limped to the bedroom door, closed it and pressed the lock, knowing full well a bobby pin or one swift kick could bust it open. But she prayed it would buy her some time. Well, praying wasn't exactly the right word.

Grabbing her jeans from the side of the tub where she had discarded them in her exhaustion, she rifled through the pockets for Patrick's business card. She never expected to be dialing the number. Certainly not hours after he had given it to her. But now she was grateful to have his cell-phone number in hand. She punched in the digits with shaky fingers.

He answered on the second ring. "Kingsley." His voice was husky with sleep. Suddenly doubt crept into her mind. A buzzing filled her ears, punctuated by a drip from the sink. Maybe the sounds had been nothing more than an old house settling in the night, the tree branches scraping against the siding.

"Kingsley," he repeated, his voice urgent this time.

"Patrick," she whispered, her voice sounding loud to her ears, echoing in the quiet confines of the bathroom, "I think someone's in the house."

"Who is this?"

"Danielle. Danielle Carson." Her heart dropped. Why had she expected him to recognize her voice?

The house stood silent. Another drip fell from the faucet. Heat flared in her cheeks. Had she overreacted to a thump in the night? Had she subconsciously sought a reason to call Patrick? No, that wasn't like her. A mental image of her cowering in the dark, a cell phone pressed to her ear, fear edging her voice floated into her mind. Humiliation stiffened her backbone.

"Maybe I overreacted—" The sound of breaking glass cut her short.

Dread, like needles of ice shot through her veins. "Someone's in the house. I just woke up. I don't know..." Fear made her ramble. "I need you." She hated the breathless quality of her voice.

"Listen to me. Are you someplace safe?"

"Locked in the upstairs bathroom."

"Stay put, I'll be right there." The line clicked.

Danielle lowered herself onto the ledge of the bathtub and splayed her fingers against the cool porcelain. *Hurry, hurry, hurry,* she repeated over and over in her head. She had never felt more alone in her life.

A new jolt of fear made her jump to her feet. *Gram.* She crept toward the door, fingers on the handle, frozen with indecision. Her grandmother slept in the bedroom across the hall. She couldn't leave her there unprotected. With trembling fingers, she flipped the lock on the bathroom door and pulled it open. The subtle rumble of the pocket door in its track made her pause. A cold draft whispered across her neck, sending a chill down her spine.

What if the intruder found her?

Standing on the threshold of the bathroom, she held her breath, listening. Nothing.

She tiptoed from the relative safety of the bathroom into her bedroom. She scanned the shadowy room, desperate to find something...a weapon. Her gaze landed on the familiar shapes lined up on her dresser, a row of swimming trophies, many draped with first-place ribbons, all dusty from years of neglect. Hurriedly, she untangled the ribbons from the tallest trophy and slid it off the dresser. Its weight felt oddly comforting in her hands. If it came down to it, could she use it? The thought made her stomach queasy.

Danielle tried to swallow, but couldn't muster enough saliva. She opened the bedroom door—the hinge was blessedly silent—and peered out into the hallway. Long shadows played tricks on her eyes. In a burst of courage, she stepped toward Gram's room. A dark form lunged toward her. A scream died on her lips. She raised the trophy with both hands over her head. The intruder was faster. Strong hands captured her wrists.

"Whoa, take it easy."

Patrick's familiar voice seeped into her brain. Her body went limp from relief. His grip eased. "I could have brained you. I thought you were the intruder." Her words came out in breathless gasps. "You scared me to death."

"I told you to stay in the bathroom," he said, his tone that of a man who expected to be obeyed. He released her wrists, apparently convinced she was no longer a threat.

"I have to check on Gram." Danielle clung to the trophy and swung away from him. She reached Gram's bedroom and switched on the light. Danielle squinted her eyes at the blinding brightness. Gram lay on her side, a hand near her face blocking the light. She stirred at the commotion.

Danielle's hand flew to her mouth and tears of relief filled her eyes.

The room was thrown into complete darkness before she had a chance to talk to her grandmother.

"No lights." Patrick stood in the doorway, his low voice contained a warning. "The side door facing the driveway was wide open."

"What is Patrick doing here?" Gram sounded confused, tired.

"Gram," she whispered, trying to temper her concern, "everything's okay. Stay here."

Patrick clutched Danielle's upper arms and leaned in, his breath whispering across her cheek. "Stay up here with your grandmother. I'll check out the house." His hard expression didn't allow any room for argument.

Sweat trickled between Patrick's shoulder blades as he made his way through the house. He was acutely aware of his surroundings.

When he reached the bottom of the stairs, he adjusted the grip on his gun. He peered around the corner to gain a better view of the kitchen. From this perspective, he couldn't see the side door.

The sound of something banging in the kitchen had him on high alert. He held his gun at the ready. All his training, all those years in Iraq, came into play. With laser-like focus, he sidled along the wall into the kitchen. A cold breeze skittered across his damp skin. The side door yawned open, the wind slamming it against the counter. Keeping close to the wall, the counters, he edged through the room, anticipating the unexpected. The wind rustled the leaves on the big oak trees in the deep yard just beyond the driveway. Patrick kicked the door shut.

He did a quick canvass of the house and was convinced whoever had been here was long gone.

When he returned to the kitchen, he found Danielle standing in the center of the room, staring at the door. "Anyone could have reached in through the broken pane and unlocked it." Her thin frame visibly trembled under the moonlight streaming through the windows. She wrapped her arms around her middle. An inexplicable urge to pull her into an embrace swept over him. He wanted nothing more than to comfort her, to tell her everything would be okay. But that wasn't his place. He had a job to do.

Maintaining professional restraint, he strode over to the door, the glass crunching under the soles of his shoes. "A lot of older homes have doors like this. I see it all the time. People don't want to believe the times have changed. Crime has no boundaries."

The sound of a quiet gasp made him spin around.

Danielle's pink mouth formed a perfect O as she buckled in pain. Patrick's arm snaked out and grabbed her. "Stop." He stretched across and flipped on the light. Shards of glass littered the floor.

"Stupid, stupid, stupid," Danielle whispered. She lifted her foot. Little drops of blood added a garish hue to the yellow-stained linoleum.

The color drained from her face. He slipped one arm around her waist and guided her toward the kitchen chair. "You okay?" She looked different from the polished businesswoman he had seen in the light of day. In cotton sweats, hair mussed from sleep and no makeup, Danielle reminded him of the girl he once knew. The tomboy next door who he had grown to care deeply about.

She shrugged and scooted back in the chair. Clutching her foot with both hands, she leaned forward for a closer look. Her face immediately twisted in disgust and she clamped her eyes shut. She sucked in a breath and lowered her foot, leaning back as if to gain some distance. "I'm not very good with blood."

"Let me." He waited for a brief second for some acknowledgment. Without opening her eyes, she nodded her acquiescence.

Patrick's hands felt warm on her icy foot. The pain was a distraction from her embarrassment. How dumb to walk across the glass-littered floor with bare feet. In her defense, it *had been* dark.

A tingling started in her fingertips and threatened to race up her arms. If she didn't get ahold of herself, her stomach would revolt and her head would be spinning in no time. Focusing on something specific outside of herself had been a little trick she had learned to rein in her panic. She glanced

47

down at her foot as Patrick pressed a paper towel to the wound to stem the flow of blood. Her stomach turned queasy.

She pressed her eyes closed again and let her mind drift. An uncharacteristic thought flitted across her brain—*I wish my toenails were polished*. A smile pulled at her lips. She suddenly felt fourteen again. Patrick Kingsley, the coolest senior at Mayport High School, was crouched at her feet tending to her injury.

A nervous giggle escaped her lips. "Remember the time we played touch football and I stepped on a prickly weed?"

Patrick lifted a brow, never taking his focus off her foot. "You howled like a banshee."

"Did not."

He lifted his gaze to meet hers. "Did too."

Danielle rolled her eyes. "Whatever."

Her attention drifted back to the gaping hole in the door, a few shards of glass poked out of the wood frame. Tendrils of panic snuffed out the brief moment of levity. "What do you think happened here?" She felt a slight tug on her foot.

"Got it." Out of the corner of her eye, she saw Patrick pinching something both translucent and smeared with blood. She knew better than to look. He seemed a tad too excited about his success.

Danielle wrestled the nausea clawing at her throat. "Can you toss it in the garbage, please?" She really needed to toughen up. She was such a wimp when it came to blood and guts.

"It's worse than it looks." Patrick stood and glanced around. "Any Band-Aids? Gauze, maybe?"

"Gram keeps a first-aid kit up there." She pointed to the cabinet over the fridge. The same place her mother had hid the liquor.

When he opened the cabinet, sure enough, he found the kit. From her vantage point, she couldn't see any liquor. Why would she? Her mother—and her vodka—had disappeared a long time ago. Exactly seven days after they had arrived in Mayport for—in her mother's words—a fresh start. Apparently *Mom* wanted a fresh start *sans* kids. The room seemed to close in around her.

She turned her focus to Patrick. His gentle touch as he cleaned her wound was a testament to the kind of man he was. Closing her eyes, she held the tears at bay. Hands down, this was the most humiliated she had felt in years.

"Sorry," he said when she flinched. His voice was soothing, calm. She felt his eyes on her. "Does it hurt?"

Danielle pressed her lips together and shook her head. Her foot didn't hurt nearly as much as her pride.

He patted her knee, much like a big brother would reassure a little sister. Lucky her, she thought drolly. She tilted her head, studying him as he wrapped her foot in gauze. His square jaw was dark with whiskers. Creases at the corner of his eyes, slightly whiter than the rest of his tanned face, suggested he smiled a lot. Over the past decade and a half he had grown from a cute boy into a handsome man. A yearning for something—a missed opportunity perhaps—swept over her. She blinked a few times, shoving aside the fleeting thought. Why waste energy exploring such useless emotions?

Patrick glanced up, a smile in his eyes. "I think you'll live."

"Good to know." She pushed a hand through her hair, realizing for the first time she had a major case of bed head. Lifting both hands, she pulled it back, wishing she had a fastener.

Patrick stood up and walked to the door. He opened it wide,

49

studying its trajectory. "I'm going to call this into the station, but I'm wondering if the wind blew it open." Something in his tone told her he was grasping at straws. He cut her a sideways glance. "Do you know if you locked the door tonight?"

Danielle searched her memory. Locking the doors had been second nature in Atlanta. But here in Mayport? "I can't be sure."

"I know this door sticks."

"It's hard to open and you really have to force it shut."

"Exactly." With a gloved hand, he cleaned the remaining shards of glass from the wood frame. "Strange." He seemed to be thinking out loud. "The door had to hit the counter pretty hard to send glass across the kitchen floor. And only this one pane broke."

"The pane closest to the lock." An unnerving thought took root. Had someone broken into the house tonight?

He turned to meet her gaze, his green eyes penetrating in their intensity. He pulled his cell phone from the back pocket of his jeans. "Let me call this in. Just to be sure."

"Okay." Her throat felt parched.

His hand came up in a hold-on-a-minute gesture as he spoke to the person on the other end of the line. Something in his eyes suggested he wasn't completely forthcoming. What was he hiding? Her eyes drifted to the broken window. A chill permeated her bones.

Chief Parker answered on the second ring, his voice gruff, presumably from sleep. "Hey, Chief," Patrick said, then he mouthed to Danielle, "I'm going to take this outside."

Patrick stepped onto the driveway. He crossed one arm over his chest, his thin shirt no match for the chilly night air, a sharp contrast to the warm spell of the past few days. "This might be nothing, but I can't take the chance." He glanced over his shoulder to make sure Danielle hadn't followed him outside.

"What's going on?"

"I'm at the Carson home."

A groan sounded across the telephone line. "And there's a problem?"

"Can't be sure. The back door was open. Might have been the wind."

"But you don't think so?" Chief Parker seemed to trust Patrick's instincts. And the respect was mutual. Upon returning to Mayport, Patrick immediately had related to his boss, also a single father of a now-grown son.

"I'm worried it's related to Jenny's activities last night." Patrick paced in a ten-foot area of the driveway, trying to keep warm and gather his thoughts.

"No way. Billy doesn't know why she was at the bar last night. She got skittish and ran off before she made a buy. Remember?" Frustration was evident in Chief Parker's tone. Getting Billy Farr, a suspected drug dealer, off the street was high on the police department's list of priorities. And having their sting operation fizzle last night had been a huge disappointment.

Patrick stopped pacing and his fingers tightened around the phone. "I don't like it. We should have never allowed Jenny to serve as a drug informant."

Silence stretched across the line. This had been a bone of contention between the men. "Jenny Carson made her own choices."

"She was backed into a corner." Patrick bit back his frustration.

"Do you need an investigative team over there?" Chief Parker cut to the chase.

"No, I've got it covered."

"Okay. And Patrick," Chief Parker said, his tone softening, "we followed protocol last night."

"I know." Patrick replayed the events in his mind's eye. Last night, from a crowded parking lot across from the bar, he had personally watched Jenny get into her car and drive home. He'd followed at a safe distance. Nothing had indicated anyone had suspected anything. He had made sure she had gotten safely into the house and locked the door behind her. He was a man of his word.

But how had Jenny ended up in a car accident *after* she'd made it home? And why did he feel like he had personally let Jenny down? A nagging guilt pricked his conscience.

"If it makes you feel any better, I'll have a car go by Billy's bar, see who's around."

"I'd appreciate it, sir. I want to make sure no one's targeting Jenny."

Something niggled at the back of his brain. Had Jenny somehow tipped her hand and become the target of a ruthless drug dealer? But why break into her home when Jenny wasn't there? His heartbeat kicked up a notch, the way it did when he was working the elements of a case, much like a puzzle, and the pieces wouldn't fit. Did Jenny have something the intruder wanted? *If there had been an intruder.*

The screen door slammed. Danielle stood in the driveway, feet stuffed in sneakers with the backs pushed down. At his questioning expression, she raised the dustpan in her hand and said, "Cleaning up the glass."

"Thanks," he said to his boss and snapped his phone shut.

"Everything okay? Is Jenny in some kind of trouble?" The moonlight reflected in her trusting eyes.

"Let me take this." He lowered his gaze and took the dustpan from her, his fingers brushing the soft, cool flesh of her hand. He flipped open the blue lid of the garbage tote and dumped the broken glass. It landed with a sharp clatter.

"You didn't answer me. What did you mean when you said you wanted to make sure no one was targeting Jenny?" Danielle came up behind him and placed a hand on his back. Its tenderness coiled around his heart, melting his resolve. He was glad his back was to her.

He straightened his shoulders and slammed the lid shut. He turned around and forced a smile. "It's standard protocol in a suspected break-in to determine why a certain house may have been targeted."

Danielle crossed her arms and lifted her shoulders up to her ears. Her teeth began to chatter. "Do you think this house was targeted?"

"You never know. Maybe with the accident someone thought the house was empty. An easy target." He couldn't reveal Jenny's involvement as a drug informant for fear of further jeopardizing her safety. Or Danielle's.

Why did he feel like a liar?

Dear God, please forgive me.

The Protector lifted his fist and drove it down onto the counter. A red cloud of anger colored his vision. "Do I have to do *everything* myself?" Spittle flew from his mouth and landed on the boy—not a man, a kid, a failure—standing in front of him.

"No, sir."

"Then where is it? Explain to me exactly why you went into the Carson home like a bull in a China shop? Did you want to get caught?" The Protector curled his fingers into tight fists and ground his teeth, resisting the overwhelming urge to pummel the kid's face.

"No, sir."

As if of its own volition, his hand came up and punched the kid in the sternum. The younger man stepped back, bent over and gulped in uneven breaths. Disgust washed over the Protector. "Oh, stop being a wimp. Stand up straight. Be a man."

The kid stood, narrowing his gaze a fraction. The Protector glared in return. "Are you defying me?"

"No, sir."

"No one defies me." He thumped the kid's forehead with his index finger. "I run this place. You understand? And if you plan on sticking around, you better shape up."

"Yes, sir." The kid squared his shoulders.

That's more like it.

The kid cleared his throat. "Give me another chance. I know I can find it."

The Protector studied the younger man's face. He had such high hopes for him. But maybe he wasn't cut out for this after all. What a disappointment. "Another chance..." he hissed. "I don't know if you deserve another chance." He lifted his open hand and watched the object of his disgust flinch. He cupped the kid's cheek and tapped it a few times gently. A deep chuckle escaped the Protector's lips. He knew psychological warfare was just as crippling as physical. Maybe more so.

"Please, please...I'll get it next time." A flash of

determination sparked in the kid's eyes. *Maybe there was hope for him yet.*

Not one for reassurances, the Protector shrugged. "I'll decide soon. But either way, if they find her phone, you're the one going down."

Chapter Five

It was midafternoon before Patrick had the back door replaced with a more secure one without a window. For good measure, he also had the deadbolts replaced on both the front and back doors. Satisfied, he offered to drive Danielle to the hospital. After last night's excitement, Gram claimed she was too tired to leave the house, content to sit and visit with a friend from the church who had stopped by. Patrick suspected Jenny's condition had taken a toll on the elderly woman.

Once at the hospital, Patrick hung back as Danielle walked into Jenny's room. She went immediately to the head of the bed and smoothed her hand across her sister's hair. The silence grew heavy between them. He searched for comforting words but settled on something else entirely. "How's your foot?"

Half of her mouth tipped in a small grin. "Fine. I was a bit of a drama queen. Show me blood and it's all over."

Patrick lifted a shoulder and smiled. "Understandable." He didn't want to admit he liked taking care of her, even if it involved a small cut, a Band-Aid and some gauze.

Danielle sighed softly, her expression growing sober. "I just don't know what to do. This feeling of helplessness is killing me." Her shoulders sagged. "There's absolutely nothing I can do for my sister."

"There's one thing..." He let the words trail off.

She narrowed her gaze at him. "What?" Frustration laced her tone. "And don't tell me prayer or I'll hit you."

Patrick lifted his hands as if to protect himself and smiled. He was rewarded with a slight curve of her pink lips before they flattened into a straight line.

"No," Danielle said before he could plead his case. "I can't pray. I'd feel like a hypocrite. I haven't prayed in years, not really. Not since Gram used to drag us to church. How can I pray now when I need something? When I ignored God all along."

"God understands." His heart went out to her. How could anyone survive tragedy without faith? His faith had delivered him from the darkest days and months after his wife had died.

She shook her head and red splotches fired on her cheeks. "How can *you* pray?" she asked accusingly. "God took your wife. The mother of your child." She nearly spat out the words as her eyes grew hard.

Patrick blinked back his shock. Her words felt like knives turning in his heart. He crossed to the window, planted his hands on the sill and stared up at the gossamer clouds floating across the brilliant-blue sky.

"I'm sorry." Her voice was heavy with regret. "I didn't mean—"

Patrick didn't turn around, but he felt her eyes on him. "When I was deployed to Iraq," he said in a measured tone, "I made Lisa promise if anything happened to me, she'd raise our daughter in a happy home. I didn't want her to waste her life grieving for me. Our faith promises us eternal life." A yearning tore through his soul. Maybe if he had been around he could have saved Lisa. Maybe he could have convinced her to go to the hospital when her headaches first started. Maybe the doctors could have stopped the bleeding if she had gone in sooner.

He shook away the thought and continued, "I miss Lisa. I miss our family. But I made her make me a promise. Made her promise to move forward with her life if anything should happen to me. I told her to trust God's plan.

"I never expected she'd be the first to die." His voice broke and he bowed his head. Taking in a deep breath, he forced himself to face Danielle. A single tear rolled down her cheek, almost breaking the thin thread of control he had on his emotions. He leaned back on the windowsill. "I'd be the hypocrite if I didn't honor the promise she made to me," he whispered, his voice husky.

Danielle bowed her head. Another tear made a trail down her cheek. He resisted the urge to go to her. To brush the tear from her cheek. To tell her to trust God. To trust him. But something kept him rooted in his spot. His words would fall on deaf ears. Danielle wasn't ready to hear any of what he felt in his heart.

Danielle sat in silence while Patrick prayed. Feelings of anxiety smothered her like an itchy wool blanket. She couldn't focus on the words of the prayer. Instead, her eyes ping-ponged around the room. To the worn tile. To the white-on-white pattern on the bedspread. To the gray curtains on the window. Anything to avoid focusing on the prayer.

As soon as Patrick finished, she said, "If you need to go, I understand. I can call a cab to get home."

"I don't mind." He seemed content to sit in quiet meditation. Even after his explanation, she still couldn't understand how his faith had helped him overcome the tragedy of losing his wife.

Soft footsteps drew Danielle's attention toward the door. A woman, no more than fifty, walked into the room. "Hello, I'm Dr. Moss." The stethoscope around her neck and white lab coat confirmed her identity.

Patrick stood and shook her hand. "Nice to see you again." He held out his palm toward Danielle. "This is Danielle Carson, Jenny's sister."

"I was hoping to talk to you today," Dr. Moss said, her tone gentle. "Sorry I was unavailable earlier, but that's what happens in a small town." She adjusted the stethoscope slung around her neck. "We don't have enough of me to go around."

The two women shook hands. Patrick gently squeezed Danielle's arm. "I'll step out so you can talk."

"I'd like you to stay." Butterflies flitted in her stomach. Only moments ago she had tried to push him out the door, yet now she clung to him for moral support.

"Actually," Dr. Moss said, giving Patrick a meaningful look, "I think it's something you should hear." The doctor flipped a paper on the clipboard, as if to double check her facts before speaking. She turned to Patrick. "What do you know about Jenny's accident?"

"Not much more than we noted the morning Jenny was brought in. Her car went off the road and hit some trees. Our traffic investigator is still combing through the details, but best we can surmise she wasn't wearing a seatbelt."

Danielle lowered her eyes, trying to shake the image of her sister's small frame slamming against the hard edges of the vehicle's interior. She exhaled a shaky breath and fought against the white lights floating in her field of vision. *Please, please, please, don't let me pass out.*

Dr. Moss apparently sensed her distress. "Do you need to sit down, Miss Carson?"

Danielle shook her head, fear rendering her speechless. Dr. Moss seemed to be assessing her with a professional eye before continuing, "Your sister has injuries inconsistent with a motor vehicle accident."

Goose bumps peppered her skin. Her sister's bruised face brought forth a new flood of guilt and fear. "I don't understand." She grabbed the smooth metal bar of the side rail, her legs going to jelly under her. She was only peripherally aware of Patrick's solid hand on the small of her back, his voice reassuring in her ear.

"Can you give me more details?" Patrick asked.

"Well, for one, most accident victims who aren't restrained have damage cross here—" Dr. Moss pointed to her midsection, "—usually where the steering wheel comes into contact..." The physician let her words trail off as she met Danielle's gaze. "I'm sorry. I know this is hard to hear."

Danielle lifted her hand, steeling herself for whatever came next. "Go on."

"Her broken nose may have resulted from the car accident, but she also has some bruising around the upper thighs. As if someone had kicked her. Repeatedly."

Danielle let out a gasp. Placing two firm hands on either side of her waist, Patrick led her to the chair by her sister's bed. Her knees bent of their own volition. "You think someone hurt my sister before she got in the car?"

"Her injuries are very suspicious. Yes." Dr. Moss studied Danielle, perhaps sensing her full-blown panic attack. "Here, have some water."

The physician's awareness only fueled Danielle's symptoms. Hyperaware, she watched Dr. Moss pour some water from the pitcher and hand it to her. She took tiny sips. Heat warmed her cheeks. The urge to run—to get out of this stifling hospital room—nearly overwhelmed her. Drawing in a breath, she locked eyes with Patrick. "You have to find whoever did this to my baby sister."

He gave her a quick nod. "Will you be okay here for a little bit? I have to make a phone call." When she didn't answer, he leaned down. "Dani?" His warm breath whispered across her cheek as he called her by her childhood nickname.

"Do what you have to do." She rested her chin on her shoulder and watched Patrick and Dr. Moss leave the room, their heads tipped in quiet conversation.

As soon as she was alone, warm tears rolled down her cheeks unchecked. Someone had intentionally hurt her sister. Had she gotten into an accident trying to flee her attacker? Why? Why? Why? She pressed a hand to her mouth as the troubling thoughts jackhammered on her brain.

Danielle shifted forward in her seat, her back ramrod straight as yet another disturbing thought took root. Had whoever hurt Jenny come back last night?

Chapter Six

"Thanks for the ride." Across the front seat of the darkened vehicle, Danielle studied Patrick's shadowed features. Not ready to go inside Gram's quiet house where she'd have to face her thoughts, she racked her brain for a reason for him to stay. A reason that didn't make her seem needy. After the physician's report, Danielle's world had gone from spinning out of control to flying off its axis entirely. Who had attacked Jenny?

Patrick covered her hand with his, warm and comforting. "We'll find who did this." His smooth voice was a salve to her nerves.

Tamping down the emotions hovering below the surface, she bit her lower lip. "We need to find who Jenny was with on Thursday night," she said, turning to stare out the windshield. Until now, she'd never given much thought to how far back from the street Gram's house sat. And how the looming trees provided the perfect cover for anyone who wanted to lie in wait.

"We're working on it." Something in Patrick's clipped answer gave her pause.

"Do you know more than you're telling me?" The moonlight glinting off the whites of his eyes revealed nothing new. She wiped her sweaty palms down the thighs of her jeans.

"I don't know how your sister ended up in the hospital. But I will find out."

"Does Jenny have a lot of friends she hangs out with? Maybe they can tell us where she was. Give us a clue."

Patrick squeezed her hand. "Let me do my job."

Danielle lowered her gaze. "I know. I'm sorry. I feel so hopeless."

Patrick ran a hand across the back of his neck. "The chief has been trying to reach his son, Jimmy. Your sister and Jimmy have been dating for a while now. He's on a fishing trip and out of cell phone range."

Danielle narrowed her gaze. "Yeah, I remember Jimmy Parker. He was kind of a tough egg, considering he's the chief's kid."

"He's all right. I know he's going to be broken up when he learns about Jenny." Patrick patted her hand. "Get some sleep, Dani." Pushing open his door, he squinted against the dome light. The faint smile on his lips didn't reach his eyes. He seemed eager to go. She tried not to take offense. He had a daughter waiting at home, but he had spent his entire Saturday helping her. She had no right to seek comfort from him. He owed her nothing and he had already given more than she deserved.

Danielle climbed out. Patrick met her around the front of the vehicle.

"Do me a favor. Make sure you lock up tight tonight."

Fear sloshed in her stomach. "Do you think whoever broke in last night will come back?" She scolded herself for how quickly she had clung to the wind-blew-the-door-open theory.

"I'm right next door. I'll keep an eye on things...and you have new locks." Patrick pressed his hand to the small of her back, guiding her to the side door. "And I'll make arrangements to get an alarm. Can't hurt to err on the side of caution."

Danielle slowed her pace, absorbing his words, not sure if his promise should make her feel secure since he'd be watching or terrified because he felt the need to watch. The sound of the leaves rustling in the wind drew her eye up to the mostly bare branches. As they rounded the front of the house, she noticed one lonely light glowed through the front window. She imagined Gram sitting in her favorite chair, either knitting or reading, or perhaps dozing.

"Well, thanks for everything," she said and gave him a quick wave of her hand as she stuck the new key into the lock.

"Mind if I walk in with you? Something in Patrick's eyes caused a flicker of apprehension to course through her.

"Is something wrong?" Her voice suddenly sounded loud in the quiet night air.

He tipped his chin toward the door. "Humor me."

The kitchen sat quiet, save for the loud ticking of the clock on the wall. She tossed her purse on the kitchen table and headed to the family room, with Patrick close behind. He scanned the surroundings. His intensity gnawed away at what little confidence she had. *What is he looking for?*

As expected, she found Gram dozing in her chair. The table lamp sent out a cone of light, pushing all the shadows into the far corners of the room. She kissed Gram's cheek and a calmness washed over her.

"Would you like some tea or something?" She didn't want him to leave but feared she had already imposed enough on his time today. Nervous bubbles flitted in her stomach as she waited for his reply. Why did it matter so much?

A small smile played on his lips. "You're exhausted." His eyes locked with hers. "Can I take a rain check?"

Affection blossomed in her chest. "Absolutely." Out of the corner of her eye, something drew her attention to the windows overlooking the darkened yard. Her heart began to beat wildly.

"What's wrong?" Patrick spun around to follow her line of vision.

She leaned toward the window. Her brain finally processed what she'd seen. It must have registered with Patrick at the same time because he reached the side door in a few quick strides. Covering her mouth, she watched Patrick grab the man who only seconds ago was yanking on the handles of the bulkhead doors leading into the basement.

A shuffling sound drew her attention toward the family room. *Gram.*

"Dear, what's wrong?" Gram's eyes glistened with worry. "You're white as a ghost. Is Jenny okay?"

"Yes, Jenny's fine. Stay here." Danielle moved toward the door. "Someone's trying to break in through the basement doors."

"What are you talking about?"

"Gram," Danielle said, "please, go back into the family room. It's safer."

Danielle wrapped her arm around her grandmother's shoulders in the hopes of guiding her away from the kitchen. What if he had a gun? Gram shrugged her off. "I refuse to slink around my own home." With her lips pinched, Gram shuffled toward the window and peered outside. "I can't see anything. It's dark out there."

A moment later, Patrick appeared at the side door with a young man, his hands cuffed behind his back. "This man says he knows you, Gram."

Danielle flipped on the kitchen light. The young man squinted and lifted a shoulder, realizing he couldn't block the light with his hands. The light reflected off an orange patch on the arm of his coat. Danielle's heart dropped. Her pulse roaring in her ears, she stepped out into the driveway and pointed her finger in the man's direction. "You were lurking in the woods yesterday morning when I was sitting on the front porch."

The young man lowered his eyes and shook his head.

"Oh, my dear," Gram said, appearing in the doorway, "please, Patrick, let him go. He's harmless. That's Henry McClure. He's Jenny's friend and does some odd jobs around the house. I called him about the old door you removed. Thought maybe he'd know someone who could use it."

"You sure?" Patrick narrowed his gaze.

"Yes. Now take off those silly handcuffs. He's not going to hurt anyone." Gram's brow furrowed and anger flashed in her eyes. Patrick seemed to regard Gram for a minute before maneuvering behind Henry and inserting the key into the handcuffs.

Henry rubbed his wrists but didn't say anything.

"What were you doing lurking around here after dark? You were trying to get into the basement," Danielle accused him. "And you were watching me from the woods the other day."

"I'm sorry, ma'am." Henry shrugged, suddenly looking like a lost little boy. "I've been busy. This is the only time I had to stop by. I thought maybe the door was stored in the basement."

Gram lifted a shaky hand. "No, Henry. I had Patrick lean it against the garage."

Henry's face scrunched up. "I guess I've had too much on my mind."

"That doesn't explain your hanging around here yesterday. Why didn't you answer me when I called to you?" Danielle's mind raced, trying to fit all the pieces together. She gestured to Henry's jacket. "I saw the orange on your coat."

One side of Henry's mouth tipped up. "I guess I shouldn't use orange duct tape to fix a tear." He twisted his mouth and scratched his unshaven jaw. "I was worried about Jenny. I didn't believe she was in an accident, and I wanted to see for myself. When I saw you on the porch—in her jacket—I thought you were her. Until you turned around. I kinda freaked. Sorry."

Or he had hoped to find the house empty, and when he didn't he had to come back at night to break in. A throbbing started behind Danielle's eyes. What was going on here? Patrick seemed to be analyzing everything the young man said. Ordinarily, Danielle relied on no one. Tonight, the knots in her stomach eased knowing Patrick was on her side.

Henry cleared his throat. "How is she? Jenny, I mean?"

"The good Lord will watch over her," Gram said, her voice remarkably confident.

"Tell her I was asking about her." Henry toed the gravel in the driveway. "Tell her I'll take good notes for her in class."

"I'll do that. Now why don't you leave the door for another day?" Gram said.

"Yes, ma'am."

Henry turned to leave. "Wait a minute," Danielle said. He turned back around. "Do you know if Jenny went out with anyone the other night? The night she was hurt?"

Henry flashed Patrick a look before quickly lowering his face. "No."

"You sure?"

Henry shrugged. "She had other things to do, but I don't know anything more. And that's the truth."

"How'd you get over here?" Patrick cut in.

"I rode my bike. If the door worked out, I was going to borrow a truck tomorrow to pick it up."

"Okay, it's been a long day," Patrick said, obviously anxious to call it a night. "I can take you home."

"No, sir. I'm fine on my bike." Henry turned on his heel and strode down the driveway to grab his bike from where he had tossed it in the shrubs. Something in his backward glance made Danielle's blood run cold.

"I worry about you in this house all by yourself." Danielle placed a hot cup of tea in front of her grandmother, trying not to think how the lacy curtain over the kitchen window gave them zero privacy. Patrick was in his police cruiser making a few calls. She was eager to learn what he'd found out about their surprise visitor.

"I haven't been alone. Jenny's been here." Gram gave her a tired smile and waved her hand. "You never had much use for this place."

"That's not true. It's just..." she let her words trail off, "...I have a life somewhere else."

"You can practice law anywhere."

"I know." She didn't have the words or strength to argue. But it was more than her job. Danielle liked the anonymity of living in a big city. Where no one knew her past. Where no one judged her because she was the poor girl who had been abandoned by her trashy mother.

Danielle longed to open up to her grandmother. Confide in her. Tell her how hard it was to be in Mayport where history cast a dark shadow. But that wouldn't be fair to Gram. Gram lived in Mayport. If Danielle rejected her roots, Gram might feel like she was rejecting her.

Gram got a far-away look all of a sudden. "Maybe I should

consider downsizing." The tremble in Gram's voice tugged at Danielle's heart. "What if Jenny doesn't come home?" She finally gave voice to what had obviously been weighing on her mind.

"Oh, Gram." Danielle rushed over and draped her arm around the older woman's shoulders, pulling her close. "Don't think like that." The same dark thought had consumed her for the past two days.

"You're the only thing I did right." Gram's small frame shook with quiet sobs. "But I can't rightfully take claim to that, can I? You were always such an independent soul." She lowered her voice. "You succeeded despite your childhood."

"You took me in. You provided the security our mom never could." Danielle pulled a tissue from her purse and handed it to Gram.

The older woman dabbed at her tears. "I never understood where I went wrong with your mother. Her dad—your grandfather—was a drunk. I finally kicked him out when your mother was a teenager. Maybe it was too late. She tended to be drawn to men just like her father. No-good men..."

"Don't blame yourself." Danielle searched for the right words. "Jenny's doing fine."

Gram shook her head. "Jenny reminds me of your mother. A troubled soul. I've been worrying about her. Even before this horrible accident."

"You don't think she'd gotten herself into any trouble?"

"I don't know." She paused, working her lower lip. "I don't think so. But she was always on the go—school, work and boyfriend. I don't know how she did it. I don't think that girl slept for more than a few hours a night."

Gram looked up at Danielle, her watery eyes glistening under the harsh kitchen light bulb. "Do you think she fell asleep at the wheel?"

That would seem plausible, if not for Jenny's other injuries. "I don't think so, Gram. But the police will figure it out." Alarm bells sounded in Danielle's head. Had Danielle been taking some sort of stimulant to stay awake? To keep up her busy schedule? She dismissed the thought. What would that have to do with her accident anyway?

Danielle slipped into the kitchen seat across from her grandmother and grabbed her hand. "Can you think of anyone Jenny might have gone out to see the night of her accident?"

Gram shook her head. "She's always home by nine to help me upstairs to my bedroom. That night was no different."

"You never heard her go out?"

"No." Gram pulled her hand free and fidgeted with the collar of her white blouse. "She tells me if she's going somewhere. She leaves me her cell phone number on my night stand. I've never had to use it. But I suppose I could have fallen asleep and she didn't want to wake me up to tell me she was leaving."

Gram flattened her hands on the table and pushed to stand up. "Once Jimmy gets home, he can tell us. He certainly kept track of Jenny's friends."

"Does she hang out with anyone besides Jimmy?"

"The poor child barely has time." Gram twisted her mouth. "I know she has a few new college friends. A study group or something. That's how she met Henry. He's such a nice boy. We probably scared him half to death tonight. Don't know what the boy was thinking coming here after dark." Gram patted Danielle's hand.

Patrick stepped into the kitchen and wiped his feet on the rug. "Henry is who he says he is. Lives on the outskirts of town with his mom and dad. No priors. Father is a piece of work. The

70

chief told me he's been out to the house once or twice for domestic issues."

Gram shook her head. "I told you the boy was harmless."

Henry's story had panned out. But something about the kid showing up at the house at night still bothered Patrick. Had Henry been trying to get into the basement? It wouldn't be outrageous to learn Billy, the neighborhood drug dealer, had recruited Henry, a kid desperate for a few bucks to pay for college. But the police had nothing to support that theory. Yet.

Patrick decided to do a little more digging before he called it a night. Billy wasn't at his bar, so Patrick had no choice but to drive to the farmhouse Billy rented in the sticks. Chief Parker would have nixed the idea of confronting Billy, but Patrick figured the only way to get any answers from this guy was directly.

Patrick parked his vehicle halfway down the long drive and walked the rest of the distance. The weak planks on the rotting porch groaned under Patrick's weight, jeopardizing his sneak approach. Staying close to the wall, he peeked into the house. A television flickered, illuminating the profile of Billy's girlfriend, Debbie Jones. He recognized her from the grocery store where she was a cashier. A playpen was shoved into the corner. Toys littered the floor. But there was no sign of Billy.

Since the young woman seemed completely absorbed in her television program, Patrick strolled the perimeter of the property, his boots sinking in the mud. The light from the house bled into the dark night, giving his sight limited distance. A boat on a trailer sat in the yard. How could Billy afford toys, yet live in a run-down house? He supposed drug dealers didn't always make the best life choices.

The deep rumble of an engine grew closer. He strode to the front walkway and waited, his hand hovering over his gun.

The bright headlights cut across his face, blinding him. Blinking, he made out the license plate of the early model Camaro. *Billy's.* The engine idled, perhaps as Billy decided his next move. Patrick knew Billy had seen the police cruiser parked in the driveway. Patrick's heart rate spiked, much as it had when he'd made his rounds over in Iraq. His mouth grew dry as his instincts kicked in.

Billy cut the engine and emerged from the vehicle. When he got close to the house, the artificial light caught his pinched features. Billy pulled his baseball cap down to shield his eyes. "What's up?" He ran two fingers across his scraggly goatee.

"How's business, Billy?"

One side of Billy's mouth cocked into a grin. "You came all the way out here to ask me about business?"

Patrick scanned Billy's hands and face. From what he saw, there were no signs he had been in a struggle or a fight. But that didn't mean anything. He could have had one of his thugs beat up Jenny if he'd gotten wind she was a drug informant.

Billy stepped onto the porch and turned around. "This is my home. You want to talk business, come to the bar." He jerked his chin toward Patrick. "I'll even buy you a drink."

"Don't drink." Patrick shifted his stance but stayed on high alert. "You still moonlighting?"

Billy adjusted his hat farther down on his forehead. "The only work I do is at the bar."

"That's what I'm worried about."

The leather on Billy's jacket creaked as he crossed his arms over his chest. "No worries, man. No worries."

"I'll be watching you."

Billy leaned a hip against the rail of the porch. "Your visit have anything to do with that nasty accident out on Route 78 the other night?"

"What do you know about it?" A throbbing started in Patrick's temple. He should have done more to protect Jenny.

Billy levered off the rail and stabbed a finger in Patrick's direction. "I'll tell you the same thing I told Chief Parker when he came nosing around the bar. I don't know nothing about that girl."

"What girl?"

"Don't play stupid. You're out here asking me if I saw Jenny Carson before her car accident." He shot a quick glance toward the house and lowered his voice. "Sure, she was at the bar. I always notice the pretty ones. But I got my own woman. I don't need to be messing with trouble. And that one's trouble."

"Why do you say Jenny's trouble?"

Billy opened his mouth then snapped it closed. He rubbed a hand across the back of his neck. "She is trouble." He jabbed a finger in Patrick's direction. "And if you're suggesting my bar overserved her that night...that maybe she ran off the road because she was drunk...well, that's garbage. You can ask anyone at the bar. Jenny's not a drinker."

Something niggled at the back of his brain. "You seem to know a lot about Jenny. You pay this much attention to everyone who comes into the bar?"

Billy shook his head, seemingly too smart to take the bait. The lock scraping in the door drew their attention. Debbie appeared in the open doorway. Her uncertain gaze shifted between Billy and Patrick.

"Hello, Officer Kingsley," Debbie said, a frown tugging at her lips. A toddler with wet cheeks rested on Debbie's hip while fingering the woman's oversized gold hoop earring. "Is

73

something wrong?"

Billy leaned over and kissed the woman. He ran a hand down the child's thick curls. "Nothing's wrong, babe. Take the baby back inside. Give me a minute."

Patrick waited until they were alone again. "Billy, you have a family now. People who count on you." Ava's sweet face floated into his mind. "It's time to be a man for your daughter. Stop gambling with their future."

"What are you talking about?" Billy's brows snapped together, a muscle worked in his jaw. "My family is the most important thing to me. I'd do anything to protect them."

"If you don't keep your nose clean, you won't be around to see that beautiful girl grow up." Patrick pointed toward the house.

"Nothing will keep me from my family. Nothing, you hear?" Billy ground out the words, his hands clenching into tight fists. "And if you're threatening me—" he gnashed his teeth as if trying to rein in his fury, "—let's just say I'm not the only one with a family."

Patrick climbed the porch steps and approached Billy. Leaning in, he smelled the cigarette smoke wafting off Billy's clothes. His breath. It was Patrick's turn to check his anger. He narrowed his gaze. "Are you making a threat?"

Billy hiked up his chin to meet Patrick's glare. "No threat, man. Just a reminder. We both have families we better look after."

Chapter Seven

Sunday morning dawned with a glorious sunrise. Sitting at her grandmother's kitchen table, Danielle stared out the window. The pewter clouds tinged with pinks and purples set a beautiful backdrop high above the trees, mostly bare save for clusters of burnt orange and yellow leaves too stubborn to succumb to the season. Danielle always loved this time of year. Yet, despite the beautiful display of nature, she felt groggy. Tired. Anxious. The myriad events that had occurred over the past few days swirled in her head. The initial shock of her sister's condition had begun to sink in. Now her methodical mind was starting to work the puzzle of it. Who would have hurt her sister?

A thought struck her. *Jenny's cell phone.* Danielle had considered looking for it the other night, but had promptly forgotten when she had to summon Patrick to investigate the late-night noises at Gram's house. Danielle jumped up from the table and ran upstairs. Standing in the doorway of Jenny's bedroom, she scanned the floor. A discarded pair of jeans, a sweatshirt, sneakers and some undergarments littered the floor.

Danielle's pulse quickened when she noticed a purse on the floor partially obscured by a corner of the floral comforter draped haphazardly over the twin bed. *Strange. Why hadn't Jenny taken her purse?* Maybe she had more than one purse,

Danielle reasoned. She crossed the room and picked it up, surprised by its weight. Blood rushed through her veins, pulsing in her ears. Releasing a quick breath, she lowered herself onto the unmade bed and loosened the drawstring cinching the purse closed. In it she found Jenny's wallet and cell phone. Her heart skittered. Why would Jenny leave without her wallet and phone? Especially her phone. At night.

She opened the phone only to discover it was password protected. She punched in a few obvious combinations with no luck. Apprehension clawed at her. Something didn't feel right. Clutching the cell phone, an idea struck. Patrick could have someone at the police department access the phone records to see who Jenny may have talked to or texted the night of her accident.

Danielle turned the pink cell phone over in her hand. *What happened to you, Jenny?*

The doorbell sounded, snapping Danielle out of her deep thoughts. She ran downstairs and peered out the window, surprised to see Henry. She pulled the door open only a foot or so, indicating she wasn't about to let him in.

Henry hiked up his toolbox. "Thought I'd come to do a few odd jobs."

Danielle narrowed her gaze. "On a Sunday?"

He lifted a shoulder. "I do it when I can. And I really could use the money."

"Everything okay?" Patrick approached with a rake in one hand. A fondness sparked in her chest at the concern in his green eyes. She hadn't had anyone looking out for her well-being in a very long time.

"Henry stopped by to do some odd jobs." She didn't bother to hide the disbelief from her voice. Only last night he was trying to get into the basement.

Henry gave a thin-lipped smile. "Morning, Officer Kingsley. Mrs. Carson gave me a list of odd jobs. Told me to get to them when I had time."

Patrick gave a quick nod. "You need to do them right now? Today?"

Henry shoved his hand in his pocket. "She knows how much I need the money. After paying for tuition and books, I'm happy to have a few extra bucks for food." He let out an uncomfortable laugh. His gaze shifted from Danielle to Patrick and back. "If you don't mind, I'd like to get this done. I had to borrow a truck today to bring my tools and pick up the door. And I have a term paper due tomorrow."

"I'm sorry, Henry, but today's not a good day." Danielle leaned on the edge of the door.

Henry's face grew solemn. "How is Jenny?" His brown eyes glistened with concern.

"She's hanging in there." Danielle didn't really know what to say.

"I'd like to see her. Do you think that would be okay?" Henry toed the rusted metal of the doorframe.

"I don't think she's up for visitors right now. But when she's feeling better, I'll let her know you were asking about her." Something about this guy seemed off. Or maybe she was being overly suspicious.

Henry nodded slowly, a hesitant look in his eyes. "Tell Mrs. Carson to call me when it's a good time. I'll pick up the door then."

Danielle watched Henry toss his toolbox into the back of the beat-up truck. After he backed down the driveway, she tipped her head toward the rake in Patrick's hand. "Planning to do some yard work?"

Patrick glanced down at the rake in his hand as if he had forgotten it was there. "Raking leaves around here is like brushing your teeth while you're eating." A genuine smile lit his eyes. "But sometimes I like to do some manual labor and let my brain relax. I equate it to thinking in the shower."

Danielle's eyes flared wide before she quickly schooled her expression. "My sister's case is wearing on you."

Patrick reached out and cupped her face, sweeping his thumb across her jaw and taking her by surprise. Briefly closing her eyes, she drew comfort from his warm touch. "I'll find out what happened to your sister. Trust me."

Butterflies took flight in her stomach. Could she really open herself to trust him? Danielle took a step back and slipped her hands into her pockets, her fingers brushing her sister's cell phone. She pulled it out. "Oh, I found this in Jenny's room. I can't believe she'd go anywhere without it." She handed it to Patrick who turned it over in his hand.

"It's password protected."

Patrick nodded slowly. "I'll have one of our tech guys look at it first thing Monday morning."

"I appreciate the ride to the hospital," Danielle said as she sat across from Patrick in his cruiser, twisting her fingers in her lap. "And thanks for taking Gram to church with you."

Danielle turned her head to stare out the passenger's window. "I haven't been to church in years." A certain sadness laced her voice, or maybe he was imagining it.

"I understand." He didn't feel it was his place to press. Not now. It wasn't his business. Yet it pained him to know she didn't have a relationship with God. To go through life without faith...well, he'd keep her in his prayers that the Lord would eventually touch her heart.

When they arrived at Jenny's hospital room, they found Jimmy Parker, Jenny's boyfriend, sitting on the edge of the bed. He pressed Jenny's fingers to his lips. Danielle froze at Patrick's side, the subtle intake of her breath barely discernible.

Suddenly feeling like a voyeur, Patrick cleared his throat. Jimmy lowered Jenny's hand to the bed as if she were made of crystal. He shifted, wiping his wet cheeks on his shoulder. His brown hair was mussed as if he had run his fingers through it a million times. His red-rimmed eyes brightened in recognition. "Hi, Officer Kingsley."

Taking that as an invitation, Patrick stepped into the room and placed his hand on Jimmy's shoulder. "You all right, son?"

"I feel horrible." Jimmy swiped a trembling hand across his cheek.

Patrick glanced over his shoulder. Danielle stood ramrod straight in the doorway, her bloodless lips pressed into a straight line.

"Why'd I go fishing?" Jimmy scratched his head, sending a tuft of hair sticking straight in the air. "If I had been here she wouldn't have been out. She wouldn't have gotten into trouble." He sucked in a quick breath. "I'll never forgive myself if she doesn't..." He glanced past Patrick and seemed to regard Danielle for the first time.

"It's not your fault." Patrick squeezed his shoulder.

Jimmy sniffed and ran his sleeve under his nose, finally composing himself.

"When did you get here?" Patrick asked.

Jimmy lifted a hand as if to dismiss the question. "A few hours ago. I drove all night once I heard." A subtle shudder seemed to course through his body. "Thank goodness I went into town to get some supplies. I checked my cell phone and got the message from my father."

Patrick clapped Jimmy on the shoulder. "You're here now. That's what counts."

Jimmy nodded, a darkness settling in his eyes. "Guilt is eating me alive."

Patrick understood that emotion all too well. Guilt and its evil twin *what if* had nearly consumed him after his wife, Lisa, died. *What if* he had been around when Lisa first started getting headaches? *What if* she had gone to the doctor sooner? *What if* could make a sane man go crazy.

Thank goodness he had his faith to pull him out of the darkness.

Patrick smiled and lifted his palm toward Danielle. "Have you met Jenny's sister?"

Jimmy's expression froze for a fraction before an uncomfortable smile tilted his lips. "High school. Junior-year Spanish class, right?"

"It was a long time ago," Danielle said woodenly. "Nice to see you again. I'm sorry it's under these circumstances."

"I'm sorry too...for you. She's your sister and all." Jimmy twisted around to face Jenny, covering her hand with his. "Don't worry. I'm back. I'm not going to take my eyes off Jenny again."

"You talk to your father?" Patrick asked, wondering if Jimmy knew the police department had used Jenny as a drug informant.

Jimmy bowed his head. The fingers on his free hand clenched, then relaxed. Anticipation charged the air. "He told me someone beat her up." Jimmy turned, revealing his profile.

A muscle twitched in his jaw. Jimmy reached over and traced the bandage covering Jenny's nose. "My beautiful girl."

"Did she tell you who she was going out with on Thursday?" Danielle asked, her voice sounding brittle. Patrick found himself holding his breath, afraid of what Jimmy might reveal.

"I didn't have cell phone reception." Jimmy's words seemed clipped. "I know she had a lot of homework. Maybe she had a study group. Maybe she met some friends out." He shook his head, his jaw firmly set.

"The police will find out who did this to her." Patrick chose his words carefully. An upset boyfriend interfering in their case was the last thing they needed. Especially since the boyfriend was the son of the police chief.

"It's just..." Jimmy hesitated, "...Jenny was stressed out. School. Work. Everything. I told her to quit. The stress wasn't worth it. I told her I could take care of her."

Danielle visibly flinched.

"I bought her a ring in September," Jimmy continued, "but she told me she wanted to finish school first." He fingered the whiskers on his chin. "Jenny's got a mind of her own."

"That's good, right?" Danielle finally spoke up. A deep pink crept up her neck and colored her cheeks.

One corner of Jimmy's mouth curled upward. "Except when her ideas conflict with my ideas."

"So, you never talked to her Thursday night?" Danielle asked, suspicion evident in her voice. Jimmy seemed to watch her closely as she strolled around to the opposite side of the bed and smoothed a hand across her sister's hair.

Jimmy narrowed his brow as if giving it some consideration. His red-rimmed eyes spoke to his exhaustion. "I did try to call but couldn't get a connection." He pushed his fingers through his thick brown hair. "I think I even texted her more than once, but she never replied." He shrugged. "Who knows if the messages went through."

"I'm afraid you're disturbing the patient." The nurse's soft voice interrupted Jimmy.

Danielle creased her brow in question.

"We have monitors at the nurses' station. Jenny's heart rate has increased." The nurse slipped her stethoscope from around her neck and pressed the end to Jenny's chest. After listening for a moment, the nurse draped the stethoscope over her shoulder. "I'm going to have to ask you to leave. She needs quiet."

Something flickered in Jimmy's dark eyes. Something Patrick couldn't pinpoint. Pain? Hurt? Guilt? "Mind if I stay? I promise to be quiet." Jimmy raised his eyebrows and pressed his hands together in a suppliant gesture.

"As long as you're quiet, I suppose it wouldn't hurt." The nurse pointed at Jimmy. "But only one of you."

Patrick lifted his arm, gesturing for Danielle to walk ahead of him out the door. Instead, she slipped her delicate, trembling hand in his. An overwhelming urge to protect her welled up inside him.

The late afternoon sun streamed through Gram's smudged kitchen window. Danielle glanced up from her cell phone. Deleting e-mails was like swinging a sword at the snakes on Medusa's head. If she got rid of one, three more popped up in its place. She blinked her eyes, trying to refocus. Tipping her head back, she pressed her fingers to her mouth. A shudder coursed through her as she recalled clutching Patrick's hand at the hospital. What had she been thinking? Pushing away from the kitchen table, she stood and stretched her arms over her head. Every nerve ending buzzed to life.

In the other room, Gram dozed, her finger keeping her place in the Bible. How many Sunday afternoons had Gram spent reading the Bible as she and Jenny did homework at the kitchen table? An emptiness—a yearning—threaded its way around her heart and squeezed. The Bible had always been Gram's constant companion, and in times of tragedy, her grandmother clung to it like a life preserver.

Danielle wished she had something to hang on to besides work and worry. The image of her hand warmly nestled in Patrick's came unbidden. She quickly shook it away.

Suddenly, her skin grew clammy and the walls closed in on her. She slipped on her jacket and stepped out onto the front porch. Filling her lungs, she zipped up her jacket against the chill. She descended the steps and retrieved a rake from the detached garage. Maybe she'd be able to work off some of her pent-up energy. Hadn't Patrick mentioned something earlier this morning about manual labor allowing his mind to relax?

Why do all my thoughts keep coming back to him?

After about an hour, despite the huge pile of leaves in front of her, Danielle hadn't made a dent in clearing the front lawn of leaves. But the repetitive work had allowed her mind to drift, but mostly between her sister and her handsome neighbor. She rolled her shoulders, easing out the kinks. Thank goodness Gram hired someone to do lawn and seasonal cleanup. She'd never be able to finish this. Her hands throbbed and her entire body ached, but it had provided a nice release for her jumbled nerves.

The cell phone trilled in her pocket, startling her. She fished it out of her jacket pocket and recognized Tina Welch's number. Her stomach clenched in response. So much for clearing her mind.

"Hi, Tina," Danielle said as something forgotten niggled at the back of her brain.

"How's your sister?" Tina's voice sounded shaky, uncertain.

"The same. Thank you for asking."

"I'm sorry to bother you on a Sunday." A deep sigh sounded over the phone line. "Maybe I shouldn't have called. With your sister and all."

"What is it, Tina?" A buzzing started in her ears.

"The bank moved the foreclosure proceeding to this Tuesday, 9 a.m." Tina broke down in sobs.

Danielle felt her shoulders droop. "You have to be kidding me," she said, more to herself than to Tina. Softening her tone, she added, "That's in two days. You should have called sooner."

Silence stretched over the line. "I tried to reach you on Friday. Your assistant told me you were out of town because your sister had been in an accident." Desperation dripped from every word.

A dull throbbing started behind her eyes. "I'm sorry I forgot to call you back. With everything going on here—"

"I didn't know who else to call."

"Don't worry. I'll be there."

"Really?" Tina's relief was palpable. "Oh, thank you. Thank you."

Danielle wrapped a palm over the top of the rake and leaned on it. She glanced at Gram's house. She felt pulled in a million directions. "Of course I'll be there, Tina. We've come this far, haven't we?"

"Do you really think Dominic and I will be able to stay in the house?" Tina's voice cracked. "It has so many memories."

Danielle tucked the rake under her arm and pinched the bridge of her nose. Dominic's expressive milk-chocolate-colored eyes flashed in her mind. She would not be responsible for allowing this darling boy and his mother to be forced out onto the street.

"I'll be there, Tina. Don't worry."

Danielle snapped her cell phone shut and stared at it for a moment. She tipped her head back and didn't know whether to laugh or cry. If she booked a flight home tomorrow night, she could get back to Mayport by Tuesday afternoon. The pile of work on her desk came to mind. Could she really return to Atlanta without checking in at the law office?

"Hello, Miss Danielle." She spun around to find Ava standing there, her bright blue eyes taking in the huge pile of leaves.

"Hello there." Danielle's eyes shifted to the neighboring house. "Does your daddy know you're over here?"

"He had to run in to work. Bunny said I should go outside and get some fresh air." She shrugged. "I'm supposed to stay within sight of the house."

Danielle gave a quick nod. "I suppose this counts."

"How's Miss Jenny?"

"Still the same."

"Oh." The little girl lowered her eyes and pushed a few leaves around with the toe of her graffiti-decorated Converse tennis shoes. "I said a prayer for her last night. And they prayed for her in church this morning."

"That was nice." Danielle didn't know what to say. She supposed it couldn't hurt. "Thank you."

"I always feel better after I pray. God is watching out for us." Ava shrugged, looking up expectantly at Danielle. "Need

85

help with the leaves?"

Danielle glanced down at her palms. The first signs of blisters marked her soft flesh. "Actually, I was thinking of calling it a day."

Ava frowned, clearly disappointed.

Danielle hated to think of sweet Ava cooped up in the house all day. "How about you jump in the leaves instead?"

Ava's eyebrows shot up. "Really?"

Danielle lifted a shoulder. In a few hours, the wind would destroy any evidence of the work she had done here. Why not let the child have some fun first? "Why not?"

Ava hesitated for only a moment before kicking her way through the pile, sending the rich smell of autumn twirling into the air. After a few times crisscrossing the pile, she stopped and looked at Danielle. "This is fun." The excitement on her face was contagious. "But maybe I should go. You're probably busy."

"Nope, I have nothing else going on tonight." Danielle leaned the rake against the tree. She charged the leaf pile, kicking up the leaves just as Ava had done. The little girl squealed in delight. Danielle smiled as bittersweet tears pricked her eyes. *She and Jenny used to play like this.* Ava hung back a second before joining Danielle. They crossed paths, then turned around and ran back toward the pile. Ava, in her eagerness, bumped into Danielle, and the child landed on her backside in the pile of leaves.

Horrified she had hurt her, Danielle extended her hand. "I'm sorry."

Ava's serious face broke into a huge smile. She dug her hands under the leaves and threw them up at Danielle. Danielle bent down and scooped up another bunch and tossed them gently over Ava.

"Looks like I've interrupted something?"

Danielle spun around. Patrick stood with his arms crossed, a smile playing on his lips. Ava scrambled to her feet and ran past Danielle. "Daddy."

Patrick planted a kiss on the crown of his daughter's head and pulled her into an embrace. "How's my Snugglebugs?"

"*Dad...*" Ava wiggled loose from his grip. Her cheeks bloomed red.

Patrick's green eyes locked with Danielle's. She couldn't read his expression, but her chest tightened, and she quickly averted her eyes. He picked a dried leaf from Ava's hair. "Does Bunny know you left the yard?"

"I can see the house from here." Ava bit her lower lip.

"You know better." Patrick's tone made the little giggly girl grow solemn. Instinctively, Danielle wanted to tell Ava it was okay but realized it wasn't her place. Ava was lucky to have a father who loved her dearly.

Ava opened her mouth to protest, but snapped it shut, apparently thinking better of it. She smiled tightly. "Thanks, Miss Danielle, for letting me jump in the leaves." She lifted her eyebrows in a way Danielle was beginning to realize was uniquely her. "If you want, I can help rake them tomorrow."

"Even I know when to surrender." Danielle smiled brightly, trying to convey to Ava everything was all right.

The little girl's brow furrowed.

"I'm going to hire someone to do the rest."

"Oh," Ava said in understanding. Suddenly her face lit up. "Can Miss Danielle come over for Sunday dinner?"

Patrick's eyebrows shot up in surprise, and then he quickly schooled his expression. "I'm sure Miss Danielle has other plans tonight."

"No, she doesn't. She told me she didn't. And Bunny always makes too much food. She's always saying she cooks for an army."

A slight curve tugged at the corner of Patrick's mouth. "Miss Danielle, would you and your grandmother like to join us for dinner?"

"Oh..." Danielle searched for an excuse in the leaves blanketing the yard.

"Please," Ava pleaded, her green eyes glowing with excitement. "Dad, come on. Tell her she has to come."

Patrick lifted an eyebrow, his eyes twinkling. "Ava's persistent. You may as well face the inevitable."

Danielle ran a hand across her hair and pulled out a leaf. "Let me clean up at least."

"Yay!" Ava jumped up and down. "Come over as soon as you can."

Patrick glanced down at his watch. "Make it six."

As she headed to put the rake away, she turned to watch Patrick walk hand in hand with his daughter to their house. She felt momentary panic. Her heart raced and her mouth grew dry. Was she actually looking forward to the evening? Or dreading it?

She had two hours to decide.

Chapter Eight

The fragrant aroma from the sauce bubbling on the stove made Patrick's stomach growl. Unable to resist, he reached for the wooden spoon, and Bunny rewarded him with a swift swat on his hand.

"Don't you dare," Bunny said, slanting him a glance. She picked up the spoon and stirred the sauce for good measure. She put the lid back on the pot before stepping away from the stove.

"Just a little taste." Patrick lifted his hand, holding his thumb and index finger an inch apart.

"You can wait for our guests to arrive." His mother glanced at the clock on the wall. The big hand had recently swept past the hour mark. "Shouldn't they be here already?" Annoyance laced her tone, making Patrick wonder if this had been such a good idea.

"They'll be here soon." Patrick slipped into the kitchen chair across from his daughter. Ava shot him a furtive glance, then went back to drawing butterflies and flowers with chalk on a piece of purple construction paper.

"I'm making a picture for Miss Danielle," Ava announced.

"I see." Patrick planted his elbow on the table and rested his chin in the palm of his hand. Ava was growing very fond of Danielle. He understood. But what would happen when she left? His daughter would be crushed. Maybe he should put the brakes on whatever it was he was doing with Danielle before anyone else got hurt. Keep it strictly business.

After all the pain his daughter had already experienced in her short life, his heart ached. He wanted to protect her from all of life's disappointments. But life didn't work that way, did it?

The doorbell chimed and Ava bolted from her seat, her art project flapping in her hand behind her as she raced for the front door. She undid the lock, tucked the paper under her arm and pulled the handle with both hands.

A crisp breeze whirled into the foyer, and Patrick grabbed the door to stop it from slamming against the wall.

"Hi, Miss Danielle," Ava bounced on the balls of her feet. "I made you something." She pressed her masterpiece against the screen door to show Danielle.

"Oh, it's beautiful." Danielle stood under the porch light, her auburn hair flowing over her shoulders, billowing in the breeze. She held a large bouquet of flowers in one hand and a covered pie plate in the other. A breath hitched in Patrick's throat.

"Let the woman in," Bunny called from the kitchen.

Feeling a little sheepish for staring, Patrick reached past his daughter and pushed open the screen door. Danielle stepped into the foyer and placed the pie on the front-hall table. Separating the bouquet into two bunches, she handed one to Ava. "Thank you for having me." Ava's green eyes lit up. Such pure joy.

Patrick glanced down at the remaining flowers in Danielle's hand. "For me?"

A smile tipped the corners of Danielle's delicate lips. She held up the pink and purple flowers. "I thought they'd match your eyes."

Ava frowned, her brow furrowing like it did whenever she got confused. "No they don't."

"I believe she's being sarcastic." Bunny approached the group, her face in a pinched expression, rubbing her forearms. "There's a chill in the air. Come in. Close the door."

Patrick pushed the door closed, brushing past Danielle as they jockeyed for position in the tight foyer. The clean scent of her hair tickled his nostrils. He lingered for the briefest of moments, enjoying the proximity.

When he stepped back, Danielle offered the flowers to Bunny, who handed them to Ava. "Child, put some water in the glass vase on the hutch and set them on the kitchen cabinet."

His daughter skipped away with the flowers, always happy to have a job of some importance.

"Gram thanks you for the invitation, but she's tired," Danielle said, wringing her hands in front of her.

"I understand. I'll send you home with a plate for her," Bunny said. "I'm sorry about your sister. We're praying for her at church."

"Thank you." Color infused Danielle's cheeks. "And this..." Danielle picked up the dish she had set down. "I brought a pie. It's one of those frozen ones you heat up. I hope it's okay. It's all I could find at the grocery store on a Sunday."

Bunny waved her hand in dismissal. "I'm sure it's just fine." Her lips curved into a small smile, but her eyes seemed flat. "I already made a dessert anyway."

The color on Danielle's porcelain cheeks grew deeper.

"We missed you at church service this morning." Bunny's perfectly groomed brow arched in disapproval. Without waiting for an answer, she added, "If I remember, your mother wasn't much of a churchgoer either."

91

"Mother, I don't imagine our guest wants to be interrogated," Patrick said.

"I'm just—"

"Bunny..." Patrick scooped the plate from Danielle's hands and angled his face away from her to give his mother his best be-good stare.

Smiling, Patrick turned to Danielle and slipped his hand in hers and led her to the kitchen. "Sorry about that," he whispered in her ear, "she has a certain charm."

"I remember." Danielle pulled free from his grasp and smoothed her hands on her jeans. He immediately missed its warmth. "Maybe my coming over here wasn't such a good idea," she whispered, her long hair brushing against his cheek. He had to refrain from reaching out, touching her hair, breathing in its clean scent. His resolve to keep her at arm's length was quickly deteriorating.

Ava popped up from where she had been collecting the vase from the bottom cabinet. "Bunny made my favorite dinner." She took in a deep breath, closing her eyes briefly. "Spaghetti and meatballs."

The spicy aroma of sauce and garlic made Patrick's stomach growl. "I hope you're hungry."

"I am." Danielle stood with her hands clasped in front of her.

"Well, go on now." Bunny stepped into the kitchen and shooed them away. "Go on now and have a seat. Dinner is about to be served."

"Can I help with anything?" Danielle asked.

"No. You're a guest." Bunny picked up a tray of garlic bread and shoved it toward Patrick. "*You* can carry this."

Once in the dining room, Patrick pulled out a chair for

Danielle, taking the opportunity to whisper in her ear, "I'm glad you made it."

Danielle looked up, a question in her wide eyes.

When Ava entered the room, Patrick asked, "Did you wash your hands?"

"Yes, Dad." The young girl seemed exasperated. She plopped down in her seat and stared across at Danielle. "Are you moving in next door?"

Danielle visibly swallowed. "No, I'm only visiting. I'll have to get back to my law practice soon."

"You keep bad guys out of jail, right?" His daughter's eyes rose expectantly. "Like on the cop shows on TV?"

Both Bunny and Patrick turned toward Ava at the same time. The young girl shrugged. "Sometimes when I'm flipping the channels I see them."

"No, not that kind of lawyer," Danielle said, a smile in her voice. Patrick tried to imagine her in a crisp black suit arguing cases in a court of law. Danielle exuded a quiet confidence she'd lacked when she was a teenager. "I work for a law firm that mostly handles corporate real estate. We help people buy and sell office buildings downtown."

Ava nodded, a tiny line creasing her forehead. "So you don't help people buy houses or anything?"

"Sometimes, but not often."

"Oh." Ava shifted toward her grandmother. "Bunny sells houses. Maybe you could move here and work in her office."

Bunny and Danielle locked eyes. Tension zinged between them. The older woman spoke first. "My office is not very exciting."

"Are you showing houses next Saturday, Bunny?" Ava asked, twisting the noodles on her fork.

"Dear, you know Saturday is my busiest day at the office."

"Maybe Miss Danielle can take me to the fall festival at church. Jenny was going to take me..." Her small voice drifted off.

"Ava, we'll talk about that later. It's a week away," Patrick said, keenly aware of Danielle's gaze on him.

"But you said you had to work and Bunny has to show houses..." Ava shifted in her seat, a pout on her lips.

Danielle shrugged. "I don't mind. One way or another, I'll be here next weekend."

"You'll be here that long?" Patrick asked, trying to keep his tone casual.

"I'll be back and forth."

Patrick nodded and watched Danielle spread her napkin over her lap. His precious daughter stabbed a meatball, a brilliant smile lighting up her face.

"Yay! I'm going to the fall festival with Miss Danielle."

Patrick's contented mood evaporated. How would his daughter deal with it when Danielle left for good?

The delicate teacup clinked against the matching saucer. "Thank you, Mrs. Kingsley. Dinner was delicious," Danielle said.

"Please, call me Bunny. Everyone else does. I'm sorry your grandmother wasn't feeling up to the company." Bunny's eyes drifted to the stairs where Patrick had ascended with his daughter to tuck her in for the night. "I'll be sure to make her a plate."

"Thank you." Danielle crossed her legs and adjusted the napkin on her lap, smoothing the soft white linen across her thigh.

94

"So—" Bunny turned her assessing gaze to rest squarely on her guest, "—how long *do* you plan on staying in town? I know how real estate is. It's not something you can be away from for long."

Danielle cleared her throat. "There are people in my office to handle my clients, if necessary." She neglected to mention Tina Welch. There was no one to help Tina while she was gone.

Bunny lowered her chin, her perfectly sculpted bob didn't move. Her lips spread into a thin line. "That's okay with you? Handing your clients over to your coworkers?"

Danielle ran pinched fingers along the edge of the cloth napkin on her lap. She imagined this was how insects felt under a microscope. "My sister needs me now."

Bunny gave her a knowing smile. As if saying, "You were never around for her before." Or perhaps Danielle was projecting her own feelings onto Bunny.

"I'll juggle everything I can until things settle down," Danielle said, searching the stairway for any sign of Patrick's return. "And I will be making a short trip to Atlanta this week."

"Really? So you don't have plans to move back to Mayport?" Bunny lifted a pale brow, skepticism etched on her features.

"No, not at all."

Bunny gave a quick nod and rose to her feet. She gathered a few plates and disappeared into the kitchen. Picking up a few dishes of her own, Danielle followed. Bunny grabbed a flowered apron from the hook near the sink and draped it around her neck. She tied it at her waist and smoothed her hands down the front.

"Dear, Ava seems to have taken a liking to you." Bunny turned on the faucet and let the water run over her fingers. "She invited you for dinner. Now she wants you to take her to the fall festival at church."

Heat crept up Danielle's neck and checks "I don't mind taking her."

"I'd go myself, but I have to work." Bunny hiked her chin with a sniff.

"I understand."

"Do you?"

Danielle opened her mouth, then shut it again, realizing Bunny wasn't looking for an answer.

"My son and granddaughter have had enough loss in their lives. They don't need you flitting in here, into their lives, then leaving when it suits you."

"I have no intention of staying in Mayport, Mrs. Kingsley—" Patrick's mother flashed her a look and Danielle immediately corrected herself, "—um, Bunny. I never pretended otherwise." Nervously, she bit her lip, then quickly schooled her expression. She felt fourteen again, trying to gain approval of the woman next door who always seemed to look down her nose at her.

Bunny grew up with Danielle's mom. Her mother's reputation colored Bunny's perception of her. She wanted to tell Bunny she was in no way, shape or form, her mother. But it didn't matter. People in a small town would think what they wanted to think. Why bother wasting her breath trying to convince Bunny otherwise? She didn't plan on sticking around anyway.

"As long as we understand each other." Bunny plugged the sink and pumped some dish detergent into the water. Thick, sudsy bubbles filled the sink. Bunny tossed a glance over her shoulder. "I'll be sure to keep Jenny in my prayers," she added, by way of dismissal.

"Thank you," Danielle whispered as tears threatened. "I better check on Gram."

"Daddy, one more kiss." Two pink-clad arms extended from a sea of stuffed animals. Ava's strong arms clasped around Patrick's neck and pulled him down, forcing him to come face-to-face with some Disney character. He never denied his only child one more hug. He was aware she was growing up, and soon she probably wouldn't give him the time of day.

He pressed a kiss to her forehead, smelling the fresh minty scent of toothpaste. "Night. God Bless."

"Dad...?" She let the word hang out there.

"Yes?" he encouraged her. His own father was distant, but his mother had made up for what his father had lacked. Inwardly, he rolled his eyes. Perhaps Bunny overcompensated, inserting herself into all aspects of his life. Regardless, he'd be forever grateful to his mother for loving her granddaughter with all her heart. Without a mother, she desperately needed a female's influence.

His mind drifted to earlier this afternoon when he'd found Ava and Danielle playing in the leaves. He hadn't seen his daughter so carefree in a long time. Had Danielle been responsible for the joy on Ava's face? Something in his heart gave way.

"*Dad?*" Ava tugged on his sleeve. "Are you listening to me?"

"Of course, Snugglebugs. What's up?'

"I like Miss Danielle."

Patrick pressed another kiss to his daughter's cheek and straightened. He studied Ava's face in the shadows. "I like Miss Danielle too."

"Do you like her like you liked Mommy?" Ava rubbed a hand across her sleepy eyes.

"I loved your mother very much."

"I know." Ava rolled over and tucked a hand under her pillow and closed her eyes. "But when you first met Mommy, you must have liked her enough to ask her on a date." Sleepy, she drew out her words. It amazed him his young daughter had such insight. A slight shiver went through him as he imagined his sweet precious daughter entering the dating world. It would have to wait until she turned twenty-one. He'd see to that.

Patrick smoothed a hand across his daughter's blonde hair. "Danielle and I were friends when we were in high school." *And I liked her very much.* But between their youth and his disapproving mother, their relationship wasn't meant to be.

Ava yawned and snuggled into her pillow. "That's nice." Her voice came out on a sleepy yawn. "Night. God Bless."

"Night." He backed out of the room and closed the door. "God Bless." Patrick found Danielle waiting for him at the bottom of the stairs with her jacket on. A twinge of disappointment rippled through him.

"Leaving already?"

"It's late."

He glanced at his watch. It wasn't that late. "Can I get you some coffee? Maybe we can have it out on the porch. It's a little chilly, but..." Patrick wasn't ready to say goodnight.

"I'm afraid if I have any more caffeine..." Danielle held out her trembling hand.

"Come on." He cupped her elbow and led her outside. "Let's just sit and talk a few minutes."

Once settled on the wicker couch, Danielle hugged her jacket to her body.

"Cold?"

She shrugged. "I think my blood has thinned out."

"Do you like living in Atlanta? We spent some time in Fort Benning. After growing up in the Great White North, the mild temperatures were a nice change."

"Yeah, but I miss a good snowstorm. There's nothing like snuggling up with a blanket by the fire with a good book while the wind howls outside, the snow piling up. The promise of the world stopping for just one day." Danielle looked up, a soft smile playing on her lips under the moonlight. She shrugged, then stood up abruptly as if remembering where she was. "I'm sorry, I'm rambling. Did you have news about my sister?"

"Not yet." He hated not being honest with Danielle. He knew far more than he could let on. It was too risky to reveal Jenny had been a drug informant. If word got out, Jenny's life would be in jeopardy. Jenny's battered body flashed through his mind. He clasped his hands and rested his elbows on his knees. "We're working on it."

"Well—" she dragged her hand along the porch railing, "—I really should go."

He reached out and took her hand, encouraging her to sit back down. "Listen," he said, "Ava can get ideas sometimes."

Silence stretched between them.

"You don't have to go to the fall festival on Saturday. She can be persistent when she wants something."

Danielle laughed. "She reminds me of Jenny at that age. Since she knew she couldn't talk my mom into anything, she'd always hit me up. With success, I might add."

"Please don't feel like you have to go." He had to find a way to put the brakes on his daughter's growing fondness for Danielle. Yet something squeezed at his heart at the thought of telling Ava she'd have to miss selling her crafts. She had worked so hard. "I'll try to get out of work early."

"Let me take her."

"You're busy."

Danielle stood and glared at him, the moonlight reflected in the whites of her eyes. "Is this you speaking or your mother?" Without waiting for an answer, she strode toward the steps.

Patrick followed her down the steps. "Wait."

Danielle spun around. "I'm not good enough to keep your daughter company?"

He jerked his head back. "What? I never said that."

Unshed tears shimmered in her eyes as she jutted her chin out in defiance. "You didn't have to."

Patrick raked a hand through his hair. He turned and stared toward the street, then back at Danielle. Something in his heart shifted. "You're not talking about my daughter. You're talking about me. Us."

She snorted. "There was never an *us*. Just a foolish little girl."

"You were just a girl. You had to carve out your own life. Go to college." He lifted his palm toward her. "You're a successful lawyer."

She crossed her arms and ground her teeth.

"You would have resented me. You needed to spread your wings." He stretched out his hand, daring to stroke her smooth cheek with his fingers, but she stepped back, out of his reach.

"You never gave me a chance." She lowered her gaze.

Patrick moved closer and tilted his head, trying to see into her eyes. "We were kids."

"You got married the very next year." Danielle's eyes narrowed.

"I was being deployed."

She lifted her hands in a surrender gesture. "I don't care

anymore. It's not relevant to my life now." She pointed at him. "I am taking Ava to the fall festival. I am not going to disappoint that little girl. I'd never do that to her."

She spun around and Patrick caught her arm. "Please, don't leave mad."

Danielle froze and shook her head. Tears on her cheeks glimmered under the white light. He swept his thumb across the wetness and cupped her cheek. Her breath hitched. That was all the invitation he needed. Lowering his face, he brushed a kiss across her soft lips. The heat of the contact sent a keen awareness flowing through his body.

Danielle's dark lashes swept her fair cheeks. She let out a shaky breath. Her eyes snapped open and she grabbed his wrist, forcing his hand away from her face. She shook her head and took a few steps backward. "I can't." She spun around to leave.

"Wait, I know Bunny fixed a plate for Gram," Patrick said, hoping Danielle would stay long enough to calm down.

Danielle shook her head. "I made Gram dinner before I left. Thanks anyway." Her voice cracked. "I really have to go." She lifted her hand in a quick wave and ran across the yard.

A wind whipped up, sending a chill down his spine. He glanced around as an uneasy feeling dogged him. What was he doing? Rooted in place, he watched until he saw lights come on in Danielle's home. She was safe.

He supposed that's all that mattered for now.

Chapter Nine

Danielle's heart jackhammered when she saw Patrick's police cruiser in Gram's driveway. Had something happened to Jenny? Or Gram? Fear welled up in her throat. She climbed out of the cab and handed the fare to the driver through the open window, nearly missing his hand in the exchange. The hundred-dollar bill would more than cover the fare plus tip.

Without a backward glance at the departing cab, Danielle strode across the gravel, immediately annoyed with herself for leaving Mayport for her trip to Atlanta. At the last minute, the bank had postponed Tina Welch's foreclosure hearing until next week. The urgency of the trip had been lost before the landing gear of the Boeing 747 had hit the tarmac at Hartsfield International. Even though she had been gone less than twenty-four hours, it had been a total waste of time.

A whisper of dread coursed through Danielle's veins as she approached the door. The brisk autumn air did nothing to cool her fiery cheeks. She grabbed the cell phone from her purse and blinked at the display. No calls from Gram or Patrick. Surely someone would have called if there had been an emergency.

Danielle found Patrick and Gram in the living room. Patrick sat on the footstool holding Gram's hand, talking in a low voice. The side-table lamp hadn't been turned on despite the gathering darkness of the overcast day. Something in the tableau made her heart plummet. "Did something happen to Jenny?"

Patrick spun around at the sound of Danielle's voice. The dim light cast unreadable shadows in his eyes. Hands planted on his thighs, he pushed to his feet. As he walked toward her, a smile spread across his lips, sending a rush of relief through her body. Her breath came out in *whoosh*.

"Jenny is fine. She regained consciousness. But she doesn't remember anything." Patrick squeezed her hand and a jolt shot up her arm, from both relief and his gentle touch. Immediately her mind took her back to the other day, to Patrick's gentle kiss. Her flesh still tingled at the memory...and the embarrassment. Why had she overreacted and run off? What a fool. It was just a kiss.

Jenny was okay. The words finally registered. Danielle threw her arms around his neck and hugged him. Pure joy filled her heart. "Thank goodness." She came down off her tiptoes and gave him a meek smile. Ignoring the heat warming her cheeks, she brushed past him and knelt next to Gram's chair. She pulled her into an embrace.

"God is good." Gram breathed into her hair. "God is good."

Danielle pulled back to meet Gram's watery gaze. "Have you been up to see her since she woke up?"

Gram nodded and gestured behind Danielle. "Patrick took me." Her lips trembled. "She looks pale and didn't say much."

Danielle glanced over her shoulder. "She didn't say anything?"

Patrick's lips thinned into a straight line and he shook his head slightly.

Gram stroked the cover of the Bible sitting in her lap. "The nurse wanted her to rest. Said she could only have one guest."

"Jimmy?" Annoyance edged Danielle's tone. She hated the notion that Gram had been shuffled out of the room for him to sit vigil. But at least someone was there with Jenny. Protecting her.

"Jimmy. Thank God for Jimmy." Gram smiled as a tear escaped and ran down her soft cheek. "He's been there for her right along."

Guilt ran cold through Danielle's veins. Jimmy had been there. Unlike Danielle.

"Are you okay here? I'm going to see Jenny." She pulled a few tissues from the box on the table and handed them to Gram.

"I'll drive you," Patrick offered.

Danielle opened her mouth to protest but realized she didn't have a choice.

As they drove to the hospital, Danielle seemed pale and frazzled. Patrick resisted the urge to reach across the console and cover her hand to tell her everything was okay.

"How was your trip?"

She shook her head. "Not what I expected."

"You still have a job, right?" He chuckled, trying to lighten the mood.

"You laugh..." Danielle stared out the windshield, a glum look on her face. "It's not funny. A senior partner questioned my commitment to the job. Two top clients have been handed over on a silver platter to a coworker who—" she clasped her hands and pressed them to her chest, "—profusely expressed his deepest concern for my sister, while at the same time his beady little eyes glistened with glee." Instead of sounding angry, she sounded resigned. "I'll be lucky if I have a job when I return for good."

"It sounds like a dog-eat-dog world," Patrick said, still feeling like a heel for stealing a kiss the other night. He had intended to keep his distance, yet had taken advantage of her vulnerability. He owed her an apology, but didn't think this was the best time to broach the subject. Sighing, he flicked the control for the directional to signal his turn into the hospital parking lot.

Out of the corner of his eye, he noticed Danielle shifting in her seat. "It is a dog-eat-dog world. But it's my world."

"A job doesn't define you." He maneuvered into a parking space and put the car in park.

"It pays the bills." She stepped out of the vehicle and slammed the door.

Patrick jogged to catch up with Danielle. "Don't you want more?"

The automatic doors whirred open. Danielle glanced over her shoulder. "I have more than I ever had growing up."

He caught her hand. She froze in her tracks but didn't meet his gaze. "That's not what I meant and you know it."

"I have everything I need." The look in her eyes conveyed a challenge.

He reached out to touch her cheek but dropped his hand before he made contact. A million different ways he could respond swirled in his brain, but any words died on his lips.

"I have a warm house, food, clothing. More than some people." She cocked a manicured brow, then spun around and strode toward Jenny's room.

"Wait up," Patrick called.

Danielle slowed her pace but didn't stop. "Dr. Moss

suggested we give your sister another day before we start asking questions. If she mentions something, that's fine, but she suggested we don't push it."

"Okay." The single word came out clipped. Her shoulders sagged, her bravado crumbling. "Are you sure she didn't say *anything* about the accident?" He hated the implication he wasn't being forthcoming. Guilt pinged his conscience. Was he?

He cleared his throat. "She can't remember anything."

She slowed outside her sister's room. "That's not unusual with a head injury, right?" She kept her voice low. "Maybe her memory will improve?"

"Give it time." Danielle's hopeful expression pained him. "Come on." With a hand to the small of her back, he guided her into Jenny's room. Danielle sucked in a quick breath.

Jenny was lying in the bed, her white skin made paler by the white linens. Yellowish-brown crescent-shaped bruises marred the flesh underneath both eyes. Jimmy sat at the head of the bed running a strand of Jenny's hair through his fingers. His pain was palpable. Without turning, Jimmy whispered, "She's sleeping."

Patrick sensed the disappointment flowing through Danielle.

"I don't think you should wake her," Jimmy said, his voice husky with emotion.

Danielle bowed her head and Patrick moved his hand over her back in circles. "It's good. She needs her rest."

Jimmy moved away from the head of the bed and lowered his voice. "Any news on what happened?" He dragged a hand through his hair, a tic working in his jaw. Patrick shook his head. Tapping his fingers on the footboard, Jimmy glanced over his shoulder at Jenny. "You'd tell me right? You'd tell me if you knew anything?"

"As best I can, Jimmy. It's an ongoing investigation."

Jimmy's lips pressed into a thin line. "It's only a matter of time before I'm on the police force." He tipped his cheek toward his shoulder. "Don't shut me out."

Patrick cupped Jimmy's shoulder. "Jenny needs you right where you are. By her side." A tightness constricted his chest. He would have done anything to be by Lisa's side when she'd fallen sick. Instead, he'd been a world away in the Middle East when his wife had died. His stomach hollowed out.

A nurse breezed into the room with a business-like expression. "I'm going to have to ask you all to leave. The patient needs her rest."

Jimmy took up his spot by Jenny's bed and picked up her hand. The nurse stood with hands planted firmly on her hips. "You're going to have to leave too. You need your rest as well."

"But—" Jimmy started to protest.

"The nurse is correct. You need your rest too." Patrick tipped his head toward the door.

Jimmy followed Danielle and Patrick out into the hallway. "You going to be okay?" Patrick asked.

"Yeah." Jimmy rubbed a hand across his chin. He looked up at Patrick. "Something's been bothering me." He flicked a glance at Danielle.

Her eyes widened, but she pointed down the hall. "I'll give you some privacy."

Once Danielle was out of earshot, Jimmy said, "My father told me you guys are trying to figure out where Jenny was headed when she got into her accident." He set his jaw. "Have you checked out Henry?"

"What about him?"

"He seems to be real interested in Jenny." A line marred

107

Jimmy's forehead. Anger flashed in his eyes. "More than just classmates or the guy who does odd jobs around the house. I questioned her about it and she admitted he'd asked her out. But Jenny insisted they were just friends." A muscle in his jaw started twitching again. "The nurse mentioned he stopped by earlier. I don't like it."

The devastation in Jimmy's voice tore at Patrick's gut. "You think maybe Henry couldn't take no for an answer?" Had Henry taken advantage of Jenny because Jimmy was out of town? Patrick twisted his lips. But wasn't it more likely that Billy or one of his thugs had caught up with Jenny?

Jimmy looked away, determination squaring his jaw. "It crossed my mind."

The Protector slipped behind a tree and twirled the unlit cigarette between his fingers. He was too smart. If anyone suspected him of being here, they'd bag and tag his cigarettes, get his DNA and get him. Eventually.

Hours had passed since Patrick and Danielle pulled out of the hospital parking lot. Hours of being patient. Biding his time. But now the time had come to act. The beauty of living in a small town was a lack of security. A lesson he'd learned time and time again. It had served him well.

He slipped a ski mask over his face. He couldn't be too careful, even though he knew the hospital was staffed with a skeleton crew this late at night. Without making a sound, he moved across the manicured grounds and stopped outside Jenny's window. It was unlocked. He hadn't gotten this far in life without having a plan.

Muscles straining, he slid the window open. Peering inside, he listened intently. The only sound was Jenny's bedside monitor. A warning sounded in his brain. He was about to make that thing go off. He didn't have time to waste.

Using his upper body strength, he pulled himself up, threw a leg over, and in one fluid motion, he was in. He stalked over to Jenny's bedside and leaned in. Close. His nose curled back, repulsed by the unwashed scent of human hair. The other night he'd understood the attraction that had led to this mess. Tonight, he was reminded of women's lesser qualities. The needier, the weaker, the frailer of the species.

"Jenny," he whispered in a sing-song voice. "*Oh, Jenny.*"

Jenny's eyes snapped open. Just then he pressed a hand down hard on her mouth to stifle whatever weak scream she could muster. Her blue eyes looked wild, but she didn't give him much of a struggle. Poor girl was probably still weak from the beating. If she'd only had the good sense to die, he wouldn't have had to risk everything by sneaking in here. He glanced over his shoulder. The curtain billowed in front of the open window.

He pressed down on her mouth and with the other hand squeezed her hand where the tubes were inserted. In the dim light, a single tear glistened in the corner of her eye. "Oh, sweet Jenny."

She struggled to shake her head against his firm grasp. The heart monitor sounded its response. His pulse spiked. Sweat beaded under the knit fabric of his mask. He'd have to make this quick.

He pulled his hand away and patted her cheek roughly. "You don't remember who hurt you. If you say anything, I'll kill your sister, your grandmother and sweet, sweet Ava."

Sheer terror filled her eyes. He pinched her nose and mouth with his black-gloved hand. Her body bucked under his grasp, but she was no match for his brute strength. Strength always won.

He closed his eyes and imagined her life slipping away. But that was not his end-goal. Not tonight. It would be too...suspicious. He had to stay the course.

The heart monitor chirped. He ripped the plug from the outlet, silencing the offending piece of equipment. It would take the nurse seventeen seconds to make it to the room from her station. Longer since she had a habit of gabbing at shift change with the other nurse in the break room at the far end of the hall.

"Don't forget. If you tell anyone what really happened to you, I'll hurt everyone you love," he whispered his final reminder.

The sharp staccato sound of running feet broke through his adrenaline high. He let go of Jenny's face. She sucked in a sharp breath and gasped as she struggled to fill her lungs with air.

His pulse roared in his ears. He pulled back the thick curtain and stepped onto the window's edge and jumped, landing in the soft dirt. He crouched, hidden behind a bush, his body pressed against the rough brick.

Three, two, one...

"What happened here?" The nurse arrived in the room just as he had anticipated. Her alarmed voice floated out to him through the open window above him.

"Bad dream," Jenny croaked out. She broke into a coughing jag.

"Did you unplug your monitor?" the nurse asked, her voice filled with reproach.

"I must have been thrashing around in my dream."

Good girl. The only worthwhile women were the ones you

could control. If they couldn't be controlled, he'd squeeze the life out of them. A bead of sweat snaked down his back. A cramp rippled through his thigh. He ached to get out of this awkward position and get this sweltering ski mask off.

"I'll give you something to help you sleep," the nurse said. Jenny must have tried to resist, but the nurse insisted. The nurse's voice grew closer to where he hid. "Who opened this window?" she asked. Above his head, the nurse pulled the window shut and fastened the lock. Suddenly he was cast in deeper shadow. The nurse had pulled the curtains closed.

To avoid detection, he waited a fraction, the damp mud seeping through one knee of his pants. Crouched over, he bolted across the dew-covered lawn and disappeared into the woods. Safely hidden in the shadows, he ripped off his mask. He savored the memory of the terror in her eyes. Jenny would keep her mouth shut.

For now.

And the first inkling otherwise, he'd snap her scrawny neck.

Chapter Ten

"Morning." The single word sounded strained as Danielle stepped into Jenny's hospital room alone.

Jenny turned her head slowly, her flyaway hair splayed against the white pillowcase. "Boy, I must have been at death's door to get you back to Mayport." Her weak smile contradicted the deep sadness in her eyes.

"That's not very nice." Danielle's stilted laugh echoed in the sterile hospital room. She gave Jenny a tentative kiss on the cheek. The skin on Jenny's face had turned a deep purplish green. "You really had me worried."

Jenny pressed a hand to her cheek and lowered her eyes. "Me too."

"Are you in pain?" Danielle tipped her head, trying to read Jenny's mood.

"Only when I'm awake."

Danielle caressed her sister's pale cheek. Red marks marred her sister's mouth and nose. Marks she hadn't noticed before. Goose bumps swept over her skin. "What happened here?"

Jenny waved a hand in dismissal. "I ran into the door when I got up in the middle of the night to use the bathroom."

"Call the nurse when you get out of bed." Jenny flinched

and Danielle immediately regretted her stern tone.

"I'm okay." Jenny glared at her with steely eyes. She lifted her chin, but her trembling lips belied her bravado. Tears filled her eyes and her entire body began to shake. "I want to get out of this place."

"Soon, I'm sure." Danielle glanced around the sterile room. "Hey, Gram told me you were taking early education classes." She wanted to lighten the mood. And she'd promised Patrick she wouldn't ask about the night Jenny was hurt. He had claimed it was critical that he be there to measure her response.

Jenny nodded, pressing her fingers to her temples. "Yeah. I want to be a teacher. But I'm missing all my classes. It will be impossible to catch up if I don't get out of here soon." She sighed in frustration. "It was a stupid dream anyway."

"Why do you say that? I think it's great. You can catch up. Or worse case, start again in January. I can help with tuition. You can cut back on your work hours. Gram told me you were working a ton." Danielle prattled on, searching for some connection with her little sister, searching for a way to make everything okay.

Jenny closed her eyes briefly and drew in a shaky breath. "The doctor told me I might be able to go home in a few days. I'll be fine. I'm sure you need to get back to your job."

"No. Yes...I mean..." Danielle squeezed her sister's hand. "I want to make sure you and Gram are okay first."

Something flickered in Jenny's eyes that Danielle couldn't quite identify. Pain? Fear? "I'll be fine." Jenny's lower lip quivered. "Please just go back to Atlanta. I don't need your help."

"What is it? Please tell me." Danielle moved to pull Jenny into an embrace, but her sister lifted her hand, deflecting her.

"Well," Jenny said with a forced smile, "my body aches. I feel like I was someone's punching bag." Jenny flicked a glance toward Danielle and then lowered her gaze.

"Let me get Patrick. Tell him what happened. He'll arrest whoever hurt you." Danielle felt her heart rate kick up a notch. She sensed her sister was on the cusp of sharing something with her but feared the moment was slipping away.

Jenny turned her face and brushed a tear with her shoulder. "I screwed up everything."

"What do you mean?" Danielle forced the words from a too-tight throat.

Jenny stared off in the middle distance then averted her eyes. A confused expression settled on her features. "I don't remember anything about the night I got hurt." Jenny's words sounded flat, almost rehearsed.

Danielle's mouth grew dry. If only she knew the right words to get Jenny to open up. "You don't remember *anything* from the night of your accident?"

"The doctor told me memory issues are common with head injuries." Jenny inspected her fingers then bit at the corner of her thumbnail.

Danielle sensed her sister was lying. Was she protecting someone? Was she afraid?

Racking her brain for a way to draw her sister out, Danielle strolled toward the window and pulled back the curtains. Jenny squinted against the bright sunshine and groaned.

"Oh, want me to close it?" Danielle asked.

Wincing, Jenny shook her head. "No. Maybe if the doctor thinks I'm better, she'll let me go home. Do me a favor and make sure the window is locked."

Danielle did as Jenny had asked. She returned to her

sister's side and squeezed her hand. "I don't know what's going on in that head of yours." Her light and breezy tone belied the emotions warring inside her. "I promised I'd get Patrick. He's down the hall. He wants to ask you a few questions."

Jenny tucked her hair behind each ear with trembling fingers. "Chief Parker came yesterday. I told him I don't know what happened."

"Humor me," Danielle said, slightly surprised to learn Chief Parker had already interrogated her.

Danielle texted Patrick and a few minutes later he appeared in the doorway. "Danielle, if you don't mind I'd like to talk to your sister in private."

Heat warmed her cheeks. "Of course."

With hands on either side of her, Jenny pushed her backside farther up on the bed and straightened her back. "Don't bother leaving. I don't have anything to say. I already told everyone I don't remember." Her teeth chattered and fresh tears spilled down her cheeks. "I. Don't. Remember." Her voice reached a high-pitched screech.

"It's okay." Danielle rubbed her little sister's forearm. "It's okay." She glanced over at Patrick, seeking guidance. His expression possessed a mix of compassion and confusion. Was he also trying to see beyond the bruised face and mask of denials?

Jenny lowered her head, lacing her fingers through her bangs. "It will never be okay."

"You must be getting sick of driving me back and forth," Danielle said as Patrick slipped behind the wheel of his police cruiser.

"I don't mind." He turned the ignition key, leaned back and smiled. "Where to now, madam?"

"Well," she said a little sheepishly, "I was hoping to get a swim in at the Y. Do you think you can swing by Gram's so I can grab my swimsuit first...unless it's too much of an imposition? Then I can walk home from the Y." She hoped to exercise away some of the stress.

"No problem. I can chauffeur you around town and do my patrol at the same time." His soft laugh warmed her heart. In a short time, she had gotten accustomed to his companionship. Almost like old times. Rubbing her forehead, she pushed the thought away. Nothing could turn back the hands of time.

"Thanks." Looking for a distraction, she pulled her cell phone out of her bag and noticed the missed-calls indicator. She'd never get out from under the pile of work accumulating back home. "I think a few laps will help me work out the kinks."

"Still swimming?" Patrick waggled his eyebrows. "I remember that cute red one-piece bathing suit you had to wear as part of the high school swim team."

Her cheeks warmed at the memory.

"You'd stand next to the starting block fidgeting with the straps. But as soon as you stepped up on the starting block, it was like another person took over. Cool as a cucumber."

"I had no idea you paid that much attention."

Patrick chuckled. "There are lots of things you never knew."

"In Atlanta, my building has a gym on the bottom floor," Danielle said, quickly changing the course of the conversation. "I try to hit the pool a few times a week, first thing in the morning."

"Impressive."

"When my head is underwater, I forget all my problems."

Danielle braced her hand against the door as the vehicle rocked back and forth up the rutted driveway of Gram's house.

"Do you mind if I come in and say hello to Gram?" Patrick asked as she climbed out of the car.

"Gram would love to see you." She walked ahead, keys in hand. She slowed at the door and glanced over her shoulder. "The door is open. I know I closed it."

The intense expression on Patrick's face sent a jolt of cold panic coursing through her veins. "Let me go in first." He strode into the home with Danielle following close behind. The sound from a television game show blared from the family room. Gram sat in her chair dozing.

Patrick lifted the remote to turn off the TV. Danielle grabbed the remote out of his hand. "Don't," she whispered, "she'll wake up. Trust me. The sudden quiet might startle her."

"What about the door?"

"Maybe Gram opened it to greet someone and didn't close it all the way. She's had a lot of church friends drop off casseroles since Jenny's accident." Why hadn't she thought of that before? She pressed a finger to her lips. "Wait here, I'll go grab my things and we can go."

At the top of the stairs, a rustling sounded from Jenny's room. Danielle's pulse roared in her ears. Renewed panic spread through her body and settled in her stomach. She glanced down the stairs, working her lip. Should she get Patrick? She pushed back her shoulders. Maybe the wind was dragging branches against the side of the house.

Heart beating in her ears, she took a step toward Jenny's open bedroom door. She froze. A man, his back to her, bent over the nightstand, grumbled to himself. He spun around, lifting the solid metal weapon in his hand. She took a step back and turned, twisting her ankle. She grabbed the top of the railing to break her backward fall.

Henry ran toward her with an outstretched hand. Danielle opened her mouth and screamed.

Patrick took the stairs two at a time to find Danielle with her eyes squeezed shut, an open palm lifted to protect her head. Henry stood against the wall, distress etched on his face. Patrick assessed the situation, his gaze landing on the pipe wrench in Henry's hand.

"Drop it," Patrick growled, his hand instinctively hovering over the gun in its holster.

The pipe wrench landed with a loud clatter on the hardwood floor. "I didn't do anything..." Henry's voice shook.

Patrick grabbed Danielle's forearm and brought her to her feet. "What happened here?" He put a protective arm around her. She leaned into his embrace, her trembling body warm next to his.

Her pulse leapt in her neck. "I found him—" she pointed to Henry who had flattened himself against the opposite wall, "—in Jenny's room."

Henry lifted his palms to the ceiling. "Mrs. Carson hired me to fix the bathroom sink."

Patrick's eyes dropped to the pipe wrench on the floor. "Why were you in the bedroom?"

All the blood drained from Henry's face. "I was just..." glancing over his shoulder into Jenny's room, he seemed to be searching for the right words, "...I wanted to look at the photo of Jenny. I miss her."

"I don't believe you," Danielle said, stepping away from Patrick. "Why were you really in there?"

Henry shrugged. "I told you. I had to do some repairs. A friend dropped me off."

"What's going on?" Gram's shaky voice floated up from the bottom of the stairs. "Everything okay?" She sounded out of breath, alarmed.

"Did you know Henry was up here?" Patrick called down.

Gram leaned on the post at the bottom of the stairs. "Of course I did. He was fixing that pesky drip in the bathroom."

Patrick angled his head to look into Danielle's eyes. "Okay?"

She shook her head. "No, not okay." She jerked her thumb in the direction of her sister's room. "It doesn't explain why he was in Jenny's room." Patrick realized she would be a formidable opponent in a legal case.

"I told you," Henry pleaded, lowering his eyes to his tool, then quickly lifting his head again. "Jenny and I are good friends. I just wanted to see her smiling face in that photo."

Patrick nodded toward the bathroom. "Are you done with the job?"

Henry's face brightened. "Just have to get my tools."

"Go get them and Mrs. Carson will settle up with you later."

Henry moved toward the bathroom, tossing a glance over his shoulder. "I'm sorry I scared you."

Patrick rubbed his hands up and down Danielle's arms. "I think it's time I told you something."

Danielle and Patrick followed Henry onto the front porch. As soon as Henry's friend arrived to pick him up, she turned to Patrick with accusing eyes. "I think you're letting him off too easy. He's up to something." Her nerves were still humming from the earlier fright. "He looked too guilty when I found him in Jenny's room."

A shiver raced down her spine. "I hate the cold," she muttered, yanking up the zipper on her fleece. Squaring off to face him, she narrowed her gaze and set her jaw, her mood foul. "What do you have to tell me that warrants letting that creep slither off?"

"I don't believe Henry has anything to do with Jenny's injuries."

"How can you be sure?" Her pulse beat wildly in her ears.

"The night she got hurt, the Mayport Police Department had used Jenny as a drug informant." Patrick's steady gaze met hers.

Danielle's vision became almost tunnel-like. His words sounded hollow, strange. She grabbed the railing and swayed.

Patrick's eyes grew dark with concern. "Let's get you inside." He cupped her elbow.

She jerked her arm away and shook her head, disbelief clouding her thoughts. "What are you talking about? Drugs? Does my grandmother know?"

"No, only the police department."

"Apparently not." Anger bubbled up, threatening to explode in a tirade of hurtful words. "Someone found out and hurt her. Somebody else knows." The conclusion was obvious. That's why Patrick was so quick to let Henry go.

He scrubbed a hand across his pained features. He *used* Jenny and *now* he was sorry? She bit back the angry, bitter words sitting on her tongue.

"Please come inside. Your teeth are chattering."

Danielle narrowed her gaze. "No. Tell me right here, right now. I don't want Gram to hear any of this. It would destroy her."

He ran a hand across the back of his neck and seemed to be struggling with where to start. "Chief Parker pulled Jenny over four weeks ago for talking on her cell phone."

Danielle shrugged. "Okay. What? You get a ticket for that?" Anger muddled her thoughts.

"Normally. But when she stepped out of the vehicle, she dropped her purse." Danielle felt Patrick's eyes on her as he spoke. "A bottle of pills fell out."

She shook her head while a sinking feeling washed over her. "What kind of pills?"

The corners of Patrick's mouth turned down. "Prescription drugs. A controlled substance. Illegally obtained."

Briefly closing her eyes, she drew in a fortifying breath. Drugs? What was her sister thinking? She lifted her hand slowly and covered her mouth. "No, I don't believe you." Jenny would have never abused drugs, not after living with an alcoholic mother. Never. White dots blurred her vision. She felt the color drain from her face.

"Chief Parker and the district attorney offered Jenny a deal."

"What kind of deal?" Her knees threatened to buckle underneath the weight of his revelations.

"Serve as a drug informant or risk jail time."

"Drug informant? Jail time?" None of this made sense.

"She had a substantial amount. Prescription drugs are a huge problem, even in our small town. The police department is anxious to get their arms around this problem. Chief Parker saw this as a huge opportunity to get to the dealers. And your sister agreed."

Danielle drove her balled fists into Patrick's solid chest.

"You let this happen."

Patrick wrapped his fingers around her wrists to keep her hands still. "It was ultimately her decision. She came to me. Asked me what she should do. Told me she couldn't go to jail. Gram needed her. She felt like she was finally getting her life back on track."

Danielle yanked her hands free and gave his chest a final push before spinning back around. Her vision blurred. "Why didn't she call me? I'm a lawyer. I could have helped her. Advised her of her legal rights. The police department can't do this."

"It's been done before." His stoic expression fueled her fury.

"I would have made Jenny fight the charges." The man was nothing he pretended to be. "You took advantage of her situation." Tears burned the back of her eyes, but she refused to break down in front of him.

"Chief Parker's my boss."

"You couldn't talk him out of it? She's just a kid." Her voice wobbled.

"There's a chain of command that must be followed." He paused a second as if he already felt guilty enough. But his conscience should have stopped this before it'd even begun. "Jenny's not a kid. While you were off building a career, your little sister grew up."

Danielle lifted her hands, then dropped them to her sides in fists. "I can't believe this. The Mayport Police Department used my sister as a drug informant." Her voice dropped to a threatening whisper. "Why didn't *you* tell me? Why did you make me believe that her injuries were the result of some random act?"

"The less people who know about Jenny's involvement, the better. We couldn't risk word getting out." He paused. "We still

122

can't."

"But it's already too late. Someone found out and attacked her. Tried to kill her." A chill skittered down her spine. "What if they come back?" Her hand flew to her mouth as gooseflesh peppered her skin. "They already have, haven't they? They broke into the house."

Patrick nodded almost imperceptibly. "I'm afraid they have."

Danielle clenched her hand until her nails bit into her palm. "Jenny's not safe."

He touched her forearm, an unexpected anchor in the brewing storm. "The nurses have a list of acceptable visitors. And we have the dealer, Billy Farr, under surveillance. She's safe," he said, his voice even.

"Why would they break into the house? What were they looking for?" Danielle asked.

"Drugs? Maybe they were looking for Jenny. We don't know."

"You lied to me from the beginning." Danielle's words dripped with disgust. She straightened, pushing back her shoulders. She refused to succumb to the sobs clawing at her throat. Not in front of Patrick.

Hot rage seethed under her skin. "Why didn't you protect Jenny that night?"

"We tried." The regret in his eyes was unmistakable. But she didn't care. His actions had led to her sister's injuries.

"Apparently not hard enough." Hurt and sarcasm edged her words. "What went wrong?" Danielle pinned him with a gaze, heat rolling off her skin.

"Jenny went into the bar on Thursday night. She played a few games of pool, asked around on how to make a purchase.

She got spooked before she had a chance to make a deal."

"Why would someone hurt her if she never made a drug deal?"

"To send a message."

"I have a message for *you*." She gave him a measured look. "You'll never use my sister to help you again." She pressed a palm to her forehead and a bitter laugh sounded on her lips. "I'm a lawyer and my own sister didn't come to me for help."

"I made sure Jenny got home safely that night. I followed her vehicle home. Watched her go into the house. Whatever happened to her, happened after she made it home."

"Someone must have followed you."

"We were careful, but Billy does have men working for him." He lowered his voice. "I'm afraid we couldn't watch all of them."

Danielle's eyes drifted closed and she shook her head. She yanked open the door and stepped inside. Turning, she caught Patrick's pleading gaze just before she slammed the door in his face. She turned the lock and pressed her forehead against the door. The cool wood did little to stop her head from spinning. *Jenny is involved with drugs. And Patrick had used her.*

Like all the men who had used her mother.

Chapter Eleven

The next morning, Danielle found Jenny sitting up in her hospital bed, remote in hand, flipping through the channels. Jenny looked as agitated as Danielle felt. She hadn't slept much last night. Her ears had twitched at any and every bump in the night. Thank goodness they'd had an alarm system installed. But still, daylight hadn't come soon enough. And even though she didn't relish confronting her sister, it beat watching the digital clock mark time with painful accuracy.

Jenny finally flicked a gaze her way, but only for a second. The television proved more interesting. Finally Jenny spoke, her voice even. "Patrick told you." She gestured toward her with the remote. "And you have that look..." Jenny wrinkled her nose, "...disgust? Disappointment? Maybe a mix of the two with a little dash of superiority tossed in. The same way you used to look at Mom when she came home with alcohol on her breath." Jenny aimed the remote at the television, turning the volume up.

Danielle ripped the remote from her sister's hand and tossed it across the room. It crashed against the wall. The batteries rolled in opposite directions across the gray tile.

"Hey, *why* did you do that?"

"*Why* do you want to ruin your life?"

"Like Mom?" Jenny said, cocking an eyebrow, a smirk on

her lips.

Danielle leaned a hip against the foot rail and crossed her arms. "You were only ten when Mom left. I thought maybe you wouldn't..." She let her words trail off. Tears burned the backs of her eyes.

Jenny hitched a shoulder. "Some things you can't escape."

Danielle let out a long breath, unsure of where to begin. "Why would you go down the same path?"

Jenny flung the covers back and swung her legs over the edge. She batted away Danielle's offer of assistance. "I don't need your help...or your lecture. Save it."

"What *were* you thinking?" Danielle pressed her fingers to her temple, hating the shrill sound of her voice. *Keep it together. Stay in control.*

Jenny stretched her bare toes until they reached the floor. She put weight on one foot and winced. Glaring at Danielle, she refused her help a second time. "Excuse me. I have to go to the bathroom."

Sucking in her breath, Danielle reached out again and touched Jenny's knee. Her little sister froze at the edge of the bed and pressed her lips into a thin line. "Don't you see? I was doing everything in my power not to be like Mom. I just couldn't do it all. I needed help."

"By taking drugs?" Danielle asked, disbelief crowding her thoughts.

"I needed a little something to keep me going." Jenny bowed her head. "It was stupid. I know."

"Who attacked you, Jenny?"

Rubbing her temples, Jenny shook her head. "I don't remember." Her sister pushed off the bed, seeming to take each step gingerly. Danielle fisted her hands and turned away. She crossed the room and pushed the power button on the blaring TV. A few minutes later, Jenny emerged from the bathroom and crossed the room to look out the window.

"Patrick is going to find out who did this to you. He can protect you." She lowered her voice. "We are not going to stop until whoever did this is arrested."

"I just want to move past it. Let it go. Move on," Jenny said, her voice cracking.

"No. We can't let them get away with it." Anger bubbled in Danielle's belly.

"Hey, they're letting me go home today," Jenny said, changing the subject. She turned around slowly and shook her head. "I don't want to fight. I was dumb. I made a huge mistake..." She lifted her palms.

"I don't want to fight either." Danielle sensed a tentative truce. "So...they're letting you go home?"

"Finally." A tired smile tipped the corners of Jenny's mouth. "Jimmy's bringing me some clothes."

"You should have called me." Of course she had called Jimmy. A nagging guilt hounded her. Why would she expect her sister to rely on her when she hadn't been around?

"Jimmy was here when the doctor told me I could go home," Jenny said, a hint of annoyance tinged her tone.

Danielle lowered her voice. "Does Jimmy know?"

Jenny's eyes flared wide. "About the drugs?" she whispered. "No." She glanced toward the door. "No," she said more emphatically, a pleading—a fearful—look in her eyes. "And he can't know. He's trying to get into the police academy and if..." She set her jaw. "Don't you dare tell him."

Danielle let out a long breath. "Are you telling me his father is the chief of police, and you don't think he knows?"

Jenny shook her head. "Chief Parker promised me he wouldn't tell him." Her shoulders sagged. "Don't you understand the mess I've made? I couldn't risk jail time. Who would take care of Gram?" Jenny's words tumbled out one on top of the other. "And if I jeopardize Jimmy's chances of getting into the police academy..."

Danielle's cheeks warmed. Her little sister had been carrying the weight of the world on her shoulders, and she had been too busy with her own life to know it.

"I got..." Jenny shook her head in resignation, "...I got caught up in everything. Between school and my job, I couldn't keep up. A friend gave me this drug that gave me more energy. He told me it was a real prescription." She lowered her gaze. "I guess I was naive. I didn't realize it was illegal to have drugs that a doctor hadn't prescribed specifically for you."

"Which friend?"

Jenny looked at her sister, then away. "I don't want to get him in trouble. He feels bad enough. And he has his own problems to deal with."

"Tell me. Please."

Her sister's ears grew red. "Henry."

Tugging at the collar of her confining turtleneck, Danielle pinched her lips together, fearful she'd explode and say something to put a permanent wedge between her and her sister. She *knew* Henry was up to no good.

"Please, Danielle. This is my mess. Henry's struggling to get through school too. He's got a lot going on at home. You understand, right? We had the same mom. Well—" she lowered her eyes, then lifted them to meet Danielle's gaze, "—his mom works 24-7 and his dad is a drunk. They'd kill him if they found out."

"Why does it have to become your problem?"

"He's a good kid caught up in a bad situation. I want to help him so he doesn't get trapped."

Jenny's words cut to Danielle's core. "Do you feel trapped?" Her heart beat wildly while she waited for the answer.

Her little sister looked up but didn't say anything. She pressed her hand to her mouth and shook her head. "I made a huge mistake." Her words came out muffled. "I have no one to blame but myself."

Jenny walked over to the bathroom. As she pushed the door open, she said, "I'm going to brush my hair. I think it's time you went home to Atlanta."

Danielle stood staring at the closed bathroom door, a million thoughts going through her head.

Footsteps drew her attention toward the door. Jimmy strolled in wearing loose jeans and an oversized sweatshirt. "Hey, is she ready?" He tossed a small backpack on the bed.

Before Danielle had a chance to answer, the bathroom door flew open. Jenny shot her sister a subtle warning glance.

Jenny's shaky fingers fluttered across her bruised cheek. "We have to wait for Dr. Moss to sign the discharge papers." Jenny suddenly seemed jittery. Didn't she trust Danielle to keep quiet about the drugs? Or did she fear Jimmy had overheard their conversation?

"I thought you said you were ready?" Jimmy's forced laugh grated on Danielle's nerves. "I brought you clothes."

The light seemed to dim from Jenny's eyes. "I am." She opened the backpack and pulled out a T-shirt and jeans. "But we have to wait for the doctor."

Flopping down into the chair, Jimmy sneered. "Whatever..."

"It shouldn't be long." Something about the way her sister kowtowed to Jimmy set Danielle's teeth on edge. As the child of a woman who had centered her life around men, how had her sister fallen into the same trap?

Jimmy pouted in the chair, tapping his foot on the dated tile, his foot kicking one of the remote's batteries. He leaned over and scooped it up. "What's this?"

"Nothing. I dropped the remote," Jenny said. Her boyfriend gave her a skeptical look.

Danielle tipped her head toward the door. "Jimmy, you can go. I'll wait here with Jenny and bring her home."

A hopeful look blossomed on Jenny's face, or had Danielle imagined it?

"I'll bring her home," Jimmy said, as if it were the end of the discussion.

Apparently sensing an argument, Jenny moved toward Jimmy and sat on his knee. "I'd like Jimmy to bring me home." Smoothing his hair off his face, she planted a kiss on his exposed forehead. Their mother had placated an irate boyfriend the exact same way. Nausea clawed at Danielle's stomach.

Some things you can never escape.

"Okay," Danielle murmured, "I'll see you at home."

On Saturday morning, Patrick watched Ava like the proud father he was. His ten-year-old spread out an orange tablecloth, then lined up brown doilies—thanks to Gram—in a creative pattern for her fall festival display. Every time he offered to help, she shooed him away. What would he know about decorating a crafts booth?

He greeted the crafters as he paced the blacktop in front of their tables displaying everything from doll clothes to Christmas wreaths. The sun was shining and the temperature was moderate, a perfect day for the church's fall festival. So why did this uneasiness dog him? He glanced toward the parking lot. No sign of Danielle.

Patrick hadn't spoken to her since she'd slammed the door in his face the other night. She had ignored his calls. He dragged a hand through his hair and let out a long breath. He'd known using Jenny as a drug informant was a bad idea, but he'd had no idea the negative domino effect it would have on his life and everyone's around him.

His stomach clenched. Would Danielle be a no-show? He glanced at his watch. He had to get to work.

"What do you think, Dad?" Ava asked, snapping him back to the moment. Her enthusiasm lit her beautiful face as she stood back and admired the display of knit scarves, hats and slippers.

"You and Gram were busy."

Ava giggled. "It was fun. And we're going to make money for the Mayport Food Pantry."

Patrick smoothed a hand across Ava's soft curls. His little girl was growing up before his very eyes. "Did you tell Miss Danielle what time to be here?"

"I told Gram." Shrugging, Ava tugged at a doily under the stack of hats. "She'll be here."

Patrick's heart tightened. His daughter still had blind faith in people. What would happen if Danielle let her down today? And what would happen when his daughter's attractive new friend left Mayport for good? Ava would be heartbroken.

He was a fool for remotely thinking something could develop between them. The more time he spent with Danielle, the more time he wanted to spend with her. Being with Danielle reminded him of a simpler time when they were both kids. Before life's responsibilities weighed in on them. Maybe that was what drew him to her. Inwardly, he laughed. He didn't have to worry about that anymore. Danielle had made her feelings crystal clear when she'd slammed the door in his face.

"Wow! Look how beautiful."

Patrick turned on his heel at the sound of Danielle's voice, his insides tightening with an attraction he summarily dismissed. She strode toward them, her hair cascading down her shoulders, a smile on her pink lips. She passed by him with barely a glance, but he found he couldn't take his eyes off her. Ava's face broke into a wide smile, and she rushed to meet her new friend and wrapped her arms around her waist.

"Did you make all these things?" Danielle reached over and picked up a blue scarf that matched her eyes. "And look—" Danielle opened the brown bag she was carrying, "—I thought you could sell these cookies too. Everyone likes chocolate chip cookies." There was a hint of doubt in her voice.

"Thank you, Miss Danielle. Bunny also made shortbread." She took the bag and pulled out the individually wrapped cookies. Patrick's heart warmed. Danielle had gone through a lot of trouble for his daughter.

He picked up a cookie and peeled back the cellophane wrapper. "You made these?"

"Of course," Danielle said, fixing a smug look on her face, "with a little help from the tube of cookie dough from the freezer section." Her blue eyes sparked with amusement. A longing welled up from somewhere deep inside. Perhaps his daughter wasn't the only one getting too attached.

Patrick shook the thought away and took a bite. "Not bad."

"You did a great job decorating this booth." Danielle stepped back and seemed to take it all in. "Sorry I was a little late. I wanted to make sure Jenny and Gram were set for the day."

"I'm so excited Jenny is home. Maybe I can stop by and visit her later?" Ava's face glowed with excitement.

"She wanted to run over when Jenny came home from the hospital, but I told her we needed to give her a few days to rest," Patrick said. The wait had been equally hard on him.

"I'm sure Jenny would love to see you." Danielle flicked a glance in Patrick's direction. A small smile tipped the corners of her pink lips. "As long as it's okay with your dad, maybe you can stop over tonight."

He nodded and returned her smile. Hope filled his chest. Maybe she was going to forgive him after all.

Danielle turned her attention back to the booth. "Did you set everything up yourself?"

Ava nodded and smiled. "Dad helped me carry stuff over, but I put everything where I wanted it."

"Very nice."

Patrick stood off to the side, watching the exchange between his daughter and Danielle, suddenly feeling like an outsider. He glanced down at his watch. "Well, if you two ladies have this covered, I'm going to work." He resisted his overprotective desire to give Danielle some last minute instructions on what his daughter could and couldn't do. But if he expected Danielle to trust him, he'd have to learn to trust her. He also had to trust his daughter. Let go a little. How else would his daughter ever learn independence?

"You'll be back in time to go on the hayride?" Ava gestured at him to get her point across.

"Absolutely." He bent down and kissed the crown of his daughter's head, inhaling the scent of baby shampoo Bunny insisted on buying. Still. It never failed to bring him back to the early days of Ava's life. Every evening when he'd been blessed to be at home with his family and not deployed in some foreign country, he had taken Ava wet from her mother's arms after her bath and had wrapped her in a fluffy towel. Once he had her in clean pajamas, he'd rock and rock her, drinking in her sweet smell, never knowing if his next deployment would be his last.

Would he ever have that sense of contentedness again?

"We're all set here," Danielle said, drawing him out of his reverie. "Don't let us keep you."

Patrick knew when he was being dismissed. When Ava went back to setting up the crafts and baked goods, marking each with a price, Patrick lowered his voice. "Are you sure you don't mind?"

"No, I don't. And if things get slow, I brought a little work." She patted the bag on her shoulder.

"Why doesn't that surprise me?"

Danielle shot him a twisted smile. She dropped the bag onto the chair behind the booth. She leaned over and scanned the prices. "Oh, I bet you could charge another five cents for a piece of Bunny's shortbread."

"You think?" Ava pulled the cap off the marker with a tug.

"Of course, it's for charity, right?"

Ava nodded and wrote the new price.

"See you around five?" Patrick took a step back.

"Bye, Daddy, and don't be late," Ava said without turning around.

Danielle glanced over her shoulder. "Have a good day."

Patrick turned on his heel and headed toward his cruiser. Staring through the windshield at Ava and Danielle, he was certain they could be mistaken for mother and daughter based on how they laughed and huddled together to organize the booth.

A mother for Ava. The thought floated unbidden into his

head, or perhaps it had been right on the fringes since she'd walked back into his life. He couldn't deny the pull of attraction. But he had more than himself to think about. He had Ava. As he watched Danielle drape an arm around his daughter as they admired the finished booth, he couldn't deny the obvious. Danielle—for good or bad—had worked her way into their lives in a short time.

Too bad he and Danielle had such different values and goals. They didn't even have the luxury of taking it slow. To see if their relationship would blossom naturally. She'd be back in Atlanta soon. And after everything he'd done, he didn't deserve the chance to convince her they could have a future together.

Danielle shifted positions on the wooden fold-up chair, unaccustomed to sitting in one spot all day. As the day grew long, she found herself searching the crowd for Patrick's face. Even though a little piece of her heart longed to see him, she reasoned her true concern was for Ava. If Patrick was any later, his daughter would miss the hayride.

She had enjoyed Ava's company as the two of them worked on knitting projects—something she hadn't done in years—between selling merchandise. Gram had taught Jenny and her how to knit when they were little girls. Other than her sore backside, Danielle was surprised at how content she felt. She found it oddly relaxing. More relaxed than she'd felt in...well, she couldn't remember when.

As if to taunt her, her cell phone rang from somewhere deep in her purse. She reached in, recognized the number and hit the ignore button. Let her coworker John leave a message. He was probably working all weekend to cover both her projects and his. A subtle hint of guilt crept into her consciousness, until reality hit. John would be doing everything possible in her absence to position himself front and center for the next promotion. She released a quick breath. *Ah, let him.*

"Who was that?" Ava yanked the purple fuzzy yarn from the skein, her eyes intent on her task. "Work again?" The child answered her own question. "Won't you get in trouble for ignoring the call?"

"I'll tell him I didn't have cell phone reception." Danielle leaned back in the chair and took up her knitting project, rather proud of her handiwork. She had a few inches of a fuzzy purple scarf hanging off the end of her needle.

"Won't that be lying?" Ava asked, a frown tugging at the corners of her mouth, stained a pale blue from an earlier slushy drink.

Danielle lifted her eyes to find Ava watching her intently with a real look of concern in her green eyes. It was like looking into Patrick's eyes.

Danielle bit her lower lip and lifted a shoulder. "A little white one," she offered, feeling heat creep up her neck. Her morals were being called into question by a child.

"But it's still a lie."

Danielle lowered her knitting needles and met Ava's gaze. "You're right. I'll call my coworker back on Monday morning and tell him that I was busy knitting and couldn't take his call." John wouldn't believe her anyway. The workaholic had taken up a hobby?

Ava smiled, satisfied. "My dad says the truth is the best." She lowered her voice and frowned. "Even if it gets me in trouble."

"Your dad's a smart man." Danielle worked the needle under the loop and wrapped the yarn over. Yet he had used her sister as a drug informant and then had hidden it from her.

136

"My dad works too much." Ava glanced at her watch. "He's late. I'm going to miss the hayride." Pink tinged the rims of her eyes.

Danielle's heart ached for the little girl. It was going on six and her father had promised to be here by five. She wondered how often Patrick had left his daughter waiting due to his job obligations.

Broken promises and dashed hopes had been mainstays of Danielle's childhood. She had never known her father, and her mother was temperamental at best. As a child, she'd arrive home from school and slowly walk up the drive, scanning the yard and house for any clues. A million worries occupied her mind. Would her mother be home? What kind of mood was she in?

And even worse than her mother home, drunk and in a bad mood was her mother home, drunk and in a bad mood *with* her boyfriend of the month.

"Do you think my dad will be here soon?" Danielle snapped back to the moment and glanced down into Ava's questioning eyes. Despite Patrick's faults, Ava was blessed to have a father who loved her more than anything else in the world.

She smoothed Ava's curls. "I really don't know, sweetie. I'm sure he got caught up with work." Her stomach did a little flip. Had he uncovered new information on Jenny's case?

Ava shrugged and stuck out her lower lip. "Nothing new."

"I could take you." Danielle glanced down at all the crafts and cashbox sitting on the table. "But we'd have to pack up."

Ava huffed in frustration. "It will take too long. The hayride stops soon."

"I don't know what to tell you. Do you think Bunny is almost done showing houses?"

"No," Ava said, with a resignation reserved for people twice her age. "She takes forever." She craned her neck to search for her father in the crowd.

"Maybe he'll make it," Danielle murmured as she picked up the knitting needles, but she had suddenly lost interest in the project. Her eyes scanned the crowd. Nervous energy had her tapping her foot. Where was Patrick?

Out of the corner of her eye, she saw Ava yanking on the yarn. "I heard Bunny arguing with Dad when you first came to visit. She didn't think it was a good idea if I hung out with you. I don't understand why. You're really nice."

Danielle lowered her knitting. "Your grandma means well."

"But you *are* so nice."

Ava's comment made her heart swell. "You seem surprised."

"I heard Bunny say you were bad news."

Danielle shook her head. "I was when I was a teenager."

Ava's eyebrows shot up. "Really?"

Danielle pointed at Ava. "Don't get any ideas. Your dad is a police officer, remember?"

A look of dejection settled on the child's face.

Danielle squeezed Ava's knee. "I made a lot of bad decisions when I was a kid because I didn't have any positive role models in my life. Until Gram."

Ava drew her brows together.

"Don't look so serious." Danielle tweaked Ava's nose to lighten the mood. "But you have lots of positive people in your life and I expect you to make lots of good decisions. Promise?"

Ava's face brightened.

"Hey, Ava," a girl about Ava's age with black hair twirled in a messy bun called out. "You going on the hayride?"

Ava flicked a glance toward the parking lot. Danielle's stomach tightened. "I'm supposed to wait for my dad."

"But the last wagon is loading now." The girl lifted her palms.

"I can't leave all this stuff. And my dad's not here." Red splotches blossomed on Ava's porcelain skin. Tears threatened in the corners of her eyes. Danielle's heart was breaking.

Danielle stood and offered her hand. "Hello, I'm Danielle Carson."

"Hello, I'm Kayla. Ava and I are in the fifth grade together." The young girl looked her in the eye and shook her hand.

Danielle was pleasantly surprised by the girl's manners. "Kayla, who is going with you on the hayride?"

Kayla gestured over to a teenager, an older version of the girl standing in front of her, who smiled and waved. "My sister's with me." She had the typical teenage uniform that Danielle had seen over and over today. Blue jeans, a fleece jacket, fuzzy boots and a cell phone pressed to her ear.

Danielle fought an internal battle. Patrick was extremely protective of his daughter. But all Ava wanted to do was go on a hayride on the path winding through the woods separating the church and the school grounds.

Danielle gestured to the older girl. She smiled, flipped her phone shut and walked over. "Hello," she said, "can Ava go with us on the hayride?"

"Are you going with them?"

The girl tipped her head and smiled. "Sure."

"She thinks the man driving the wagon is cute," Kayla said, waggling her eyebrows. Her older sister gave Kayla a playful nudge with her hip.

"Listen, I'll take them if you want to stay at the booth," the sister offered. Watching the two young sisters interact made Danielle wistful.

Ava grabbed Kayla's hand and jumped up and down, anticipating Danielle's agreement.

"You'll stay with them?" Danielle asked, the last of her resolve evaporating.

"Absolutely," Kayla's sister said.

Danielle turned to Ava. "Okay, I'll start packing up the booth. You guys come back here as soon as you're done."

Ava's head bobbed, her green eyes glistening with excitement. "I'll come right back as soon as the ride is over."

"Okay. Go have fun."

The two girls ran off toward the hayride, their hands clutched and their arms swinging between them. A yearning tugged at Danielle's soul. She didn't know if she felt envy, regret or simply pure longing for something she'd never had. A childhood.

Sitting in his office at the police station, something niggled at the back of Patrick's brain, but he couldn't put a finger on it. He didn't believe in hunches. He put faith in his God-given talents to figure out the pieces of the puzzle. He had swung by Billy Farr's house, knowing he wasn't there. He had hoped to get some information from his girlfriend, Debbie, but either she truly didn't know anything about Billy's drug activities or she was too afraid to talk.

Tapping his pen on the desk, he mentally sorted through all the data. He had gone through the report on Jenny's failed attempt at making a drug buy and the accident report filed by

Chief Parker yet again. He could probably recite them both by heart. How did Billy Farr play into this? Was his girlfriend covering for him? Why did Jenny leave the house after he'd made sure she got safely home? Closing his eyes, he leaned back and clasped his hands behind his neck. It didn't add up.

"Sleeping on the job?"

Startled, Patrick opened his eyes to find Chief Parker standing in the doorway. Dressed in jeans and a paint-stained sweatshirt, he dragged his hand through his hair.

"Doing some work on the house?"

"Does it ever end? I finished painting the exterior and now it's time to paint the interior." Chief Parker's frown accentuated the deep lines marring his face. "I was heading home from the hardware store and I saw your vehicle in the lot."

"This case bothers me." He tapped his pencil on the file in front of him.

Chief Parker furrowed his brow. "We'll get Billy Farr. He'll screw up eventually." He stepped into the small office and rested a hip on the edge of the desk. He dragged the top sheet of the accident report toward him and flipped it around to read it. He paused for a second as if thinking. "We'll get him."

Chief Parker lifted his finger as if he had remembered something. "Jenny's cell phone was a dead end."

Patrick narrowed his eyes. "Really? The tech gave it back to you?"

"Beauty of being the boss. I put a rush on it."

Patrick scratched his head. "No late-night texts or phone calls inviting her to go out?"

"Unfortunately not. A few calls from Jimmy's number, but he already told us he tried to reach her when he was on his fishing trip." He tipped his head toward his office. "Let me go get

141

it. You can return it to Jenny."

Chief Parker retrieved the cell phone from his office and handed it to Patrick. "What was the password?"

Chief Parker hitched his shoulder. "Don't know. It's no longer password protected though."

Patrick clicked a few buttons on the phone. He looked up to find his boss watching him. "No texts the day she was attacked."

"Seems that way."

"Isn't that strange?"

Chief Parker frowned. "Nothing surprises me anymore."

"Okay." Patrick mulled over the new piece of information. "Let's see what we do have. We sent this young girl out on a mission to buy drugs and a few hours later she's beaten to within an inch of her life." He ran a hand across his chin.

"Then she ends up in a motor-vehicle accident," Chief Parker said, staring off in the middle distance. He had a knack for solving some of the toughest cases. He was methodical. Ordered. Liked everything in its place. Probably why he got to where he was today.

"Perhaps Jenny was attacked at home and bolted from the house." His boss ran through a possible scenario, "And in her hurry, she forgot her shoes. Maybe she was being chased. Lost control of the car."

"We canvassed all the neighbors." Patrick tried to poke holes in the chief's theory. "One neighbor mentioned a barking dog, but she didn't see anything."

Chief Parker turned on his heel and moved toward the door. "It's a remote area. It's dark. A pretty treacherous place to drive off the road. That barking dog saved her life. If the neighbor hadn't called it in, Danielle would be planning a funeral now."

A knot twisted Patrick's insides.

Chief Parker pushed off the corner of the desk and turned around. "What if she wasn't driving? What if she was already unconscious and Billy staged the car accident? Wanted to hide the fact she was beaten up?"

Patrick glanced down at the paper in front of him. *What if...?* It was an intriguing thought.

Chief Parker strummed his fingers on the top of the credenza. "You'll figure it out." He gave his fingers a final tap. "I'm going home." His boss tossed a glance over his shoulder and his tone lightened. "I'm surprised you're not at the fall festival."

A jolt shot through Patrick's system. He jumped to his feet. He tossed the pencil on top of the papers. He shook his head. "I promised Ava I'd be there by five." He glanced at the clock in the bullpen area that housed a mix of clerks, officers and dispatchers. *Six fifteen.*

"Well, my friend—" Chief Parker clapped Patrick on the shoulder as he squeezed by, "—you're going to be a little late."

"Lock my office, please, Chief," Patrick hollered over his shoulder as he headed toward the door.

"Lucky for me you're married to your job. And Patrick..."

Patrick hesitated, his palm on the push bar of the glass door, itching to get on the road.

"Make sure you keep me in the loop. I got a call from Debbie Jones. Told me you were out at Billy's place."

"Just trying to turn over as many leads as I can."

"Be careful. Billy Farr is a dangerous man. The last thing we want to do is tip him off that Jenny Carson is working for us."

Chapter Twelve

Patrick turned into the busy church parking lot at exactly 6:23. He jammed the gearshift into park and jumped out of his vehicle. He scooted around the sawhorse blocking traffic from the driveway now lined with crafts booths. He didn't like to take advantage of his police-officer status, but he figured this was an emergency, even if only in his daughter's eyes.

"Hello, Officer Kingsley."

Patrick tipped his hat at a young woman. "Have a nice day at the festival?" he asked.

"Gorgeous day. God always seems to bless us with good weather."

Patrick smiled and continued maneuvering through the crowd. The scent of chili, candied apples and fried dough made his stomach growl. He loved this time of year. When Lisa was alive, from the time Ava was a baby, he'd strap her on his back and they'd go hiking and admire the fall leaves.

A yearning tugged at his soul. He rarely took time for that now. Too busy with work. Or maybe he avoided the things both he and Lisa had enjoyed, fearing it would be too painful. But it wasn't fair to deprive Ava of things she had once shared with her mother. It would be like giving her a little piece of her mom back.

When he finally got to Ava's booth, Danielle was standing

with her back to him, packing up the booth. He paused a moment, taking her in. She was far from the tomboy he had known as a teen. Although she was dressed casually in jeans, she had an air of sophistication. Her deep-blue knit shirt, her coordinating blazer and leather boots were probably purchased at some high-end boutique in Atlanta. It made him wonder, not for the first time, about her life there. Would she ever consider making a change?

First things first, buddy. You'll have to get her to forgive you first.

Apparently sensing him, she turned on her heel. A small smile played on her lips. "How long have you been standing there?"

He arched a brow. "Just walked up."

Danielle went back to packing up the merchandise. "You should be proud of your daughter. She sold most of the items she made." She tapped the box next to her. "Only a few items left." She laughed, her blue eyes flashing brightly in the setting sun. Something he refused to acknowledge hit him square in the heart.

He mentally gave himself a shake. "Sorry I'm late." The little frown Ava made when she was disappointed flashed through his mind. "Is Ava mad?"

Danielle folded the flaps down on the cardboard box and leaned her elbows on it, meeting his gaze. "Of course she was disappointed. What little girl doesn't want to spend more time with her dad?" A certain coolness laced her words.

Intended or not, her words sliced him to the core. Patrick tipped his head, hoping his visor would shield his eyes.

Danielle approached him and placed her hand on the forearm of one of his crossed arms. The heat of her touch radiated through him. Meeting her gaze, he expected to find reproach. Instead her eyes were soft with compassion. "I'm sorry. I should learn to keep my mouth shut."

He covered her hand with his and squeezed. "You didn't tell me anything I haven't told myself." *A million times.*

"Don't beat yourself up." Danielle pulled her hand free and leaned back against the table, bracing her arms behind her. "I know you're working hard on Jenny's case. You're committed to your job." She lifted her shoulders, then let them drop. "Even if I don't agree with your tactics—" she obviously meant using Jenny as a drug informant, "—I understand you have a job to do."

A gust of wind picked up and her golden auburn hair blew across her face. A strand got caught at the corner of her mouth. He resisted the urge to brush it away. Did Danielle really think she and her family were simply another case?

"I'm glad." That's all he managed to say. "And I'm sorry Jenny got caught up in this mess."

"Me too." She hesitated a fraction, then angled her face up at him, her expression sincere. "Don't forget Ava's just a little girl who wants to spend time with her daddy. She's lucky to have you." Something flashed in her eyes, then disappeared. "I have to say, you're doing a wonderful job with Ava. She's great company."

"Thank you." Patrick's heart warmed. He glanced around. "Did Bunny come and get Ava?"

Danielle bit her lower lip, apprehension clouding her eyes. "I hope you don't mind, but since she had her heart set on it, I let her go on the hayride with her friend, Kayla."

"Kayla?" The name didn't sound familiar. Ava didn't bring a lot of friends home. He turned around and scanned the crowd. The last hayride had been scheduled to go out over thirty minutes ago. "And she's not back yet?" Alarm bells clanged in his head. "Did they go alone?"

Danielle narrowed her gaze and shook her head. "No, of course not. Kayla's older sister went with them." A hint of pink colored Danielle's cheeks and he immediately regretted his harsh tone. But because he was a police officer, he knew too much and often feared the worst. One of the hazards of the job.

"Wait, there's Kayla." Relief swept over Danielle's features. She gestured to a girl around Ava's age. "Kayla," she hollered, drawing the girl to the booth. "You're back from the hayride?" Uncertainty laced Danielle's voice. Patrick scanned the faces behind Kayla, hoping Ava would emerge from the crowd.

"Yeah. Thanks for letting Ava go with me. We had a lot of fun." Kayla took a bite from an apple on a stick.

"Where's Ava?" Danielle asked.

"She ran ahead to ask you for money to buy a candied apple."

"She never came back." Danielle's eyes widened

"How long ago?" Patrick asked. A muscle in his jaw twitched.

Kayla shrugged and her lower lip quivered. "At least fifteen minutes ago. I'm almost done with mine." The girl showed them her stick, the corners of her mouth pulled down. "My mom called. I really have to go. My sister went to get the car." She pointed to where the sawhorses blocked off the crafters' section from vehicles. A teenage girl waved from the window of a lime-green Volkswagen Beetle idling next to his police cruiser.

"It's okay. You go ahead." Patrick crouched down next to the girl and asked in a reassuring voice, "Where did you last see Ava?"

Kayla tipped her head toward the crowd of people. "Over by the candied-apple stand. They also have cotton candy and stuff."

"You go on with your sister."

Kayla nodded. "Thanks, Officer Kingsley." She turned and ran toward the vehicle. Patrick watched until she was safely inside with her sister.

He placed his hand on Danielle's shoulder. He felt her shiver. "It's okay. I'm sure she's fine. I'll go see if I can spot her. Wait here in case I miss her."

"Okay." Danielle seemed distracted as she searched over his shoulder. "I'll stay here. She should have been back already. Why would it take fifteen minutes?"

"Stay here." Patrick turned on his heel and headed out to find Ava. His intuition told him something was wrong.

Dear Lord, please watch over my little girl.

Danielle's eyes bounced from one face to another, all unfamiliar. Her heart jackhammered against her ribcage. Her mind whirled with the possibilities. She envisioned a big white van sliding its side door open and swallowing up poor Ava.

Her throat grew thick with emotion as she imagined one scenario worse than the next. The steady stream of people swirled in a kaleidoscope of color and random images. She felt like she was floating above herself, looking down. Her fingers tingled. *Calm down. Don't overreact.* Maybe Ava had made a pit stop to use the facilities. Yet Danielle couldn't stop the dreadful images racing through her mind.

She was on a freight train headed down the tracks to a full-blown panic attack.

She hadn't had one of those in years. The stable life she had carefully carved out for herself—unlike her mess of a childhood—had allowed her to control her life and her panic attacks. Now that she was letting others in, she remembered why she had worked so hard to keep people out. Caring too much can hurt sometimes.

"Relax," she whispered to herself as she paced back and forth in front of the booth, her eyes peeled for any sign of Ava. "Ava is okay. You're okay. Ava's okay."

A long-ago memory of Jenny and Danielle locked in a closet slammed into her mind. Huddled close, Danielle had her arm around her little sister as they rocked back and forth, fearing their mother's alcohol-fueled rage. They had offered a prayer of mercy to God. He hadn't answered. Not that night anyway. She corralled the painful image, realizing it only fueled her anxiety. She drew in a deep breath.

Calm down.

Danielle screwed up her eyes, but didn't trust the images distorted by her panic attack. She swallowed hard. Patrick strode toward her. Her heart plummeted. He was alone. *No Ava.* His hard expression did nothing to alleviate her panic. She forced a smile, trying to hide the embarrassment that always accompanied her panic attacks. One fed the other.

"Did you find Ava? Maybe she stopped by the bathrooms?"

Patrick squeezed her forearm, his solid touch tamping her panic down a notch. "I haven't found her yet."

Danielle gasped.

"I'm sure she's fine. What was she wearing? Pink sweatshirt and jeans, right?"

Danielle nodded, praying her stomach wouldn't revolt. "I'm sorry I let her go on the hayride. I had no right." She pressed a hand to her forehead.

He shook his head. "She probably just got turned around.

Stay here in case she comes back this way. Call me as soon as you see her." The look in his eyes was too painful. He had entrusted his daughter to her and now she was missing.

"Okay," she said, tiny dots starting to fill her field of vision. Slowly drawing in a breath, she strode to the far side of the booth. She found her purse and rooted through it for some bottled water.

"How did sales go today? Did Ava make a lot of money for the charity?"

Danielle spun around to find Bunny standing there in a crisp tan pantsuit. Once again, she felt the color drain from her face. But now was not the time to worry about what Bunny thought.

"Bunny, can you stay at the booth?"

Bunny's eyes flared wide. "I was going to meet some of my lady friends for some apple pie."

"I shouldn't be gone long." She had to help Patrick find Ava. She'd go crazy standing here.

Bunny narrowed her gaze. "Is something wrong, dear?"

Danielle took a deep breath. "Ava seems to be lost."

The older woman glared at her, then rummaged through her wide straw purse. "I'll call Patrick."

"He's already looking for her. I don't think it's a big deal, but I'd feel better if I could help him."

"Go, go." Bunny gestured in a shooing motion with her hands. "I'll stay here in case she comes back this way."

Danielle's shame would have been complete if she hadn't been so worried about Ava. The church grounds weren't that big. Ava was a responsible girl. If she was lost, she'd ask for help. At least she hoped so. Surely, as the daughter of a police officer, she had been schooled in basic safety protocol.

Why did you let her run off with her friends? The thought haunted her, but she shoved it away for fear another panic attack would distort her senses.

Danielle circled the Porta-Potties a few times, her eyes scanning each and every child's face. Her mouth grew dry and her heart raced. She knocked on the two occupied units. Both times, adults emerged from behind the closed doors, understandably baffled by the frantic woman on the other side.

A man with a graying goatee and a tied-dyed shirt strode purposely toward her. At first she thought he was heading toward the Porta-Potty, but he pulled up short in front of her. "Did you lose something?" he asked, a snarl pulling up a corner of his mouth revealing yellowed teeth.

Danielle felt her brow furrow. She followed his gaze. Her heart leapt with joy. Ava was crouched down making funny faces at a toddler. Danielle would have never noticed her by the stroller if the man hadn't pointed her out. The toddler's mother smiled timidly in their direction. Ava didn't seem to notice the exchange between the adults.

Danielle let out a long breath she hadn't realized she'd been holding and ran to Ava. "Honey, your father and I were worried. We didn't know where you were."

The toddler squeezed Ava's index finger. Ava wiggled it and the baby squealed in delight. "Sorry, Miss Danielle, I ran into Miss Debbie."

Danielle tilted her head, looking at the thin woman with dark circles under her eyes. "You know each other?"

The woman smiled, but it didn't reach her eyes. The man had joined them and planted his hand on the woman's shoulder. The gesture struck Danielle as more possessive than affectionate. "Sure, I see Ava at the grocery store when she comes in. I'm a cashier there." The woman hesitated. "I'm

Debbie Jones. I was in your class in high school."

Recognition slowly dawned. The woman standing in front of her was a whisper of the feisty girl she had known in high school. "Oh, yes, how are you?" Danielle feigned an enthusiasm she didn't feel.

"Fine. I still live in town and this is my little one," Debbie said.

"Isn't she the cutest?" Ava looked up, wiggling her fingers again, causing an infectious laugh to erupt from the child.

Debbie's eyes brightened with the sound.

"Miss Debbie has photos of her baby by her register. I was so excited to meet Gracie finally," Ava added.

The woman smiled shyly, her eyes cast downward. She had the fidgety movements of someone who was afraid of something. "I'm sorry if you were worried, but Gracie really seems to like Ava."

"Yeah, we didn't mean to worry you," the man finally spoke. Something in his deep, dark eyes caused the fine hairs on the back of Danielle's neck to prickle to life.

"How did you know I was looking for her?" Unease sent goose bumps across Danielle's arms.

The man tilted his head as if considering. "You called out her name?" He phrased it as half statement, half question, obviously mocking her. The whole situation unnerved Danielle. She hadn't been calling Ava's name. Something about the man seemed familiar.

"Do I know you?"

The man frowned. "Aw, I'm offended." He offered his hand and she took it tentatively. "Billy Farr. I graduated with Ava's daddy. But of course, you wouldn't know that. You only had eyes for football players." Billy pulled back his lips, making a sucking noise. That's when the name registered. *Billy Farr. The drug dealer.*

Danielle glanced down at Ava, who was thankfully too enthralled by the baby to pay any attention to their conversation.

"Come on," Danielle said to Ava, her mouth going bone dry. Holding out her hand, she drew Patrick's daughter toward her. She rested her hand gently on the child's shoulder. "Your dad's worried." She tried to act nonchalant when every bone in her body screamed that this man was pure evil.

"Don't run off so soon. We haven't had a chance to catch up." He ran his hand across his goatee. "It's a shame Jenny's all banged up. Turns out she was the party girl, huh?" He cocked a knowing eyebrow and let his gaze drift down Danielle's body, making her feel dirty. Debbie pretended she was distracted with the baby, but if her crimson face was any indication, she had heard each and every word.

"We have to go." Danielle tugged Ava's hand.

"Don't be in such a hurry. Daddy is about to join the party," Billy said.

Danielle swung around at the same time as Ava. Ava's smile brightened. "Hi, Daddy, I met Miss Debbie's baby. She's adorable."

Patrick's upper lip thinned and a muscle twitched in his jaw. "She sure is. But I'm afraid we've taken up enough of their time." He took Ava's hand and pulled her away.

As Patrick and Ava walked toward the booth, Danielle found herself rooted in place. Her head was swirling. Before she had a chance to clear it, Billy Farr leaned in close, nicotine on his breath. "Let your boyfriend know I'm not the only one with a family."

"What—" Danielle started to ask, but he held his hand up

and pivoted on the heel of his boot. In a few long strides he had caught up with his girlfriend. Danielle stared after them, trying to process what had happened.

Debbie followed Billy, her head bowed as she pushed the stroller. This woman had gone to school with Danielle and represented everything she'd feared becoming.

Chapter Thirteen

Patrick set a box of crafts on the table inside the foyer then pushed the door shut with the heel of his shoe. "I'll bring in the rest later."

"Okay, thanks, Dad." Ava slipped off her jacket and draped it over the banister. Noticing her father's raised eyebrow, she said, "I'll hang it up later."

"Okay." Patrick grabbed his daughter's hand, drawing her close. Pressing a kiss to his daughter's head, he said a silent prayer, *Thank you, Lord, for keeping my precious Ava safe tonight.* He held her for a moment longer before she pulled away.

"Dad," she said, sounding affectionately annoyed, "I'm not a baby."

Patrick planted one more kiss on the crown of her head. "I know. Can't I give my Snugglebugs a kiss goodnight?"

Ava giggled. "Night, Dad." She took a few steps toward the stairs and spun around, her thick ponytail swinging around with the motion. "Don't be mad at Miss Danielle." She lowered her gaze then lifted her bright green eyes to meet his. "I had so much fun on the hayride. And you were late," she reminded him in an accusatory tone. "But I should have come right back. I'm sorry."

"I'm sorry too. I'm glad you had fun." He crouched down in

front of his daughter and took both her hands. "I want you to be safe, that's all. My job is to protect you. And sometimes even people you think you know can be bad."

Ava's brow furrowed. "I was just playing with Miss Debbie's baby."

"I know, sweetheart. But next time, don't go off without telling someone first."

"Okay, Dad." Ava gave her father a quick peck on the cheek. With one hand, she swung around the wood banister and landed on the first stair. "*Tomorrow* can we go over and see Miss Jenny?"

"We'll give her a call," he said, noncommittally.

"Make sure you come up soon so we can say our prayers."

"Give me a few minutes."

"Okay." Ava raced up the stairs. Near the top, she grabbed the railing with both hands and leaned toward the bottom. "Make sure you thank Miss Danielle again for me. I had a really fun time today."

Patrick straightened and ran a hand across his neck. He turned around and found his mother standing in the kitchen doorway watching him, her features pinched. "I'm tired, Bunny. I'm going to fix myself dinner and hit the sack." He opened the fridge and pulled out some leftovers. Bunny took them out of his hands and busied herself preparing him a meal.

"Thanks, Mom, but I've got it."

Bunny lifted a pale eyebrow. "Let me." She tore off a piece of paper towel and placed it over the dish before she put it in the microwave. Patrick plopped down on a kitchen chair and waited for the inevitable. His mother punched a few buttons on the microwave before spinning around. She planted a fisted hand on her hip. "Now do you understand my concerns?"

Leaning forward, Patrick rested his chin in the palm of his hand. "In regard to...?"

Bunny tipped her head, giving him a pointed gaze. "You let Danielle watch my granddaughter and this happens."

"Ava is fine."

"Danielle's clouding your judgment," Bunny said, her eyes flashing with anger. "You need to distance yourself from her."

Patrick let out an exhausted sigh and chuckled. "I have a job to do. I'm investigating her sister's accident."

Bunny tilted her head. "That's all it is? A job?"

"Of course."

"Good." Bunny opened the utensil drawer and pulled out a fork and knife. "Don't let Ava get too attached. She'll be awfully disappointed when *she* leaves. And she will, you know."

Patrick scratched his head. "I appreciate your concern, Mom, but there's nothing to worry about."

Bunny shook her head and pointed at him. "You need to think of Ava. Danielle's shown today she's not a responsible adult. The apple doesn't fall far from the tree."

"That's not fair and you know it." He closed his eyes, hating to think what might have happened to Ava. Was his mother right?

"I don't know what I'd do if something happened to my granddaughter." Bunny drew in a deep breath through her nose and hiked her chin, yet her composure slipped a fraction. "Here. Eat your dinner before it gets cold." She grabbed his plate from the microwave and set it in front of him.

Patrick stabbed a potato with his fork. "Nothing's going to happen to Ava."

Bunny patted his shoulder. "I worry."

He covered her hand with his. "It's okay. There's no need to

157

worry." His stomach churned, taunting him.

Danielle's hands trembled. She climbed the back steps of Patrick's house and lifted her hand to knock when she heard Bunny's strained voice through the closed door.

"Danielle's clouding your judgment. You need to distance yourself from her."

Danielle froze. Her pulse roared in her ears. Her first instinct was to turn, leave, since she was obviously interrupting a private conversation.

She heard Patrick's deep chuckle. "I have a job to do. I'm investigating her sister's accident."

"That's all it is? A job?" Bunny's voice sounded uncertain.

"Of course."

I have a job to do. Patrick's honesty stung like a slap in the face. The wind whipped up, pushing leaves across the porch. The scraping noise made the small hairs on the back of her neck stand on edge. She glanced over her shoulder. The deep shadows in the darkened yard made it virtually impossible to see beyond the small ring of light seeping out from the Kingsley home.

The conversation inside seemed to fade away, yet Danielle paused. She glanced at the pink cell phone Patrick had returned to her only an hour ago. She was supposed to give it to Jenny. Instead, she found herself here when the only thing she wanted to do was go home, pull the covers over her head and forget this day. But she didn't have a choice. Taking a deep breath, she knocked. Patrick pulled the door open. Tufts of his hair stood on edge as if he had been dragging his hands through it.

"Come on in." He stepped back, allowing her to pass.

"I'm sorry to interrupt." More than he'd ever realize.

"You're not interrupting anything," Patrick said, giving her a tired smile.

Bunny lifted her hands. "I was just going up to bed. Night, Danielle." She gave Patrick a knowing glance before she turned to climb the stairs.

"I'm sorry. I know it's late. Has Ava gone to bed?"

"On her way. What's up?"

Danielle pressed a few buttons on Jenny's cell phone and handed it to him. Apprehension rolled over her in waves. He glanced at the message glowing on the screen.

"*Sat big nite. U need 2 make delivery—B.*"

Patrick looked up with hardened eyes. "Did Jenny see this?" He read it out loud. "Saturday big night. You need to make a delivery. B...Billy?"

"Jenny didn't see it. The phone was still in my purse when I heard it chime." She crossed her arms and drew up her shoulders, trying to stave off the cold. "I'm afraid...for Jenny." She shook her head. "The caller and number are restricted. It's not a big leap to think B stands for Billy."

Patrick glanced toward the stairs. "Let's talk outside."

Danielle followed him onto the porch. He braced his hands on the railing. His breath came out in a little puff of clouds. She hugged herself and rubbed her arms, trying to keep her teeth from chattering.

He cut her a sideways glance before returning his gaze to the yard. "We never suspected Jenny of dealing."

Danielle bowed her head, feeling her knees get weak. She must have audibly gasped, because next thing she knew, Patrick pulled her into an embrace and ran his hands in circles

159

over her back. She pressed her cheek against his broad chest and clung to him, a safe harbor in the storm. Eyes closed, she savored the fleeting sense of security, getting intoxicated by his fresh scent.

Patrick was the first one to break the silence. "I don't think Jenny's dealing. This text right now is too convenient. Someone's trying to shift the blame. Billy maybe?"

Danielle drew in a deep breath and stepped back. "There are a bunch of calls from restricted numbers over the past week on this phone. What if…" Anger bubbled up. What if her sister wasn't so innocent? She couldn't voice her suspicions.

A pained expression darkened his eyes. "I'm sorry this is such a mess." He bowed his head briefly before meeting her gaze. "I should have protected your sister the night she got hurt…" He let the words trail off. "But we have someone on Billy Farr 24-7. We'll get him. I promise."

"But what about Billy approaching Ava at the festival?" Danielle rubbed her forearms, trying to quell the tremble rioting through her.

"Ava was with Debbie and her daughter. Billy didn't show up until he found you. My officer confirmed that. He was under constant surveillance." The look in Patrick's eyes seemed to plead with her to trust him.

"I have to tell you something else. Something I promised Jenny I would keep in confidence."

"What?" Patrick's brows drew together.

Danielle let out a sigh. "Henry was Jenny's supplier. She promised me he only did it for her, because she was desperate. But now I'm not so sure."

Patrick plowed a hand through his hair. "I'll talk to him."

She placed a hand on his forearm. "Can you do it without it

looking like I betrayed Jenny's confidence. Our relationship is strained as it is. If he's just some mixed-up kid like her, I don't..." she closed her eyes and tipped her head back, "...I don't know what to do."

"Trust me. I'll handle it."

"Thank you." Danielle's eyes drifted over to Gram's house, dark except for the light glowing from the front window. A chill raced down her spine. "I don't feel safe here."

Patrick ran a finger down her cheek. His tender touch melted her resolve. "I won't let anything happen to you."

Danielle worked her lower lip. "I'm going to convince Gram to visit her sister in Buffalo for a little while." She pressed her lips together and shook her head. "I don't want her in the house...in case. But I don't think I'll be able to convince Jenny to leave."

Patrick nodded almost imperceptibly.

Her eyes locked with Patrick's. Deep inside something shifted. Could she actually trust a man? Trust this man? She nodded, as if answering her own unasked question. What choice did she have?

"You're welcome to stay here. We have an extra room," Patrick said.

Danielle tipped her head and studied the wreath of fall foliage adorning the door. When she'd first moved to town, she'd envied the warm *Leave It to Beaver* family living next door. She used to lie in bed at night and wonder what it would be like to have a mother and father and a normal house. Back then, she would have given anything to be part of the Kingsley home. But she wasn't a little girl anymore.

"Thank you, but I'll be fine. I'll set the alarm."

"Good. And I'm right next door." Patrick reached out and

stroked her cheek with his thumb.

Her eyes drifted closed at the intoxicating gesture. She sensed, rather than saw, Patrick moving closer to her. She felt his lips brush her temple before he abruptly pulled back. "Maybe when this is all over…"

Danielle blinked a few times, relishing his gentle touch more than she should have. She took a small step backward. Wrapping her arms around her middle, she tried to keep her lower lip from trembling. "Let's not kid ourselves." She spun around to face the darkened yard, away from Patrick's hurt look. "When this is all over, we're both going back to our own lives."

A disturbing thought slowly seeped into her brain. An awareness. Suddenly she was convinced Patrick wasn't the only one watching her.

The Protector cruised by the Carson house with his vehicle's lights off. He was surprised to see the light on in the front room, the shades drawn. His fingers itched. Something told him this problem wasn't going away.

Jenny was home now but didn't seem to be talking. How long would that last? If that meddling sister kept hammering away at her, she might get some ideas. She might think it was okay to stand on her own two feet. To destroy everything important to him.

He doubted her amnesia act. But how long could fear buy him silence? He couldn't take that chance.

He scrubbed a hand across his face. The minute he'd met the waif, he'd had her pegged. She acted all sweet and innocent, but he knew she was trouble. A shadow crossed behind the blind. He stepped on the gas, easing past the house. He

162

imagined her turning the deadbolt, putting on the chain. Security for the naïve. He ran a hand across the smooth steering wheel.

His gut told him his time was running out. He had unfinished business.

Chapter Fourteen

Danielle slid her cell phone across the yellow legal pad. Bowing her head, she threaded her fingers through her hair and massaged the back of her head. Great way to start the day. She let out a long breath, knowing she should be relieved her boss had approved another week's personal leave, but she wasn't. Her most important files had already been handed over to coworkers. She'd have to work ten times as hard to make up for the lost time and to prove herself again. The only bright spot was the bank had set a firm date later in the month to review Tina's foreclosure file.

"What's eating you?"

Danielle's head snapped up. Jenny stood in the doorway dressed in gray sweatpants and an oversized Mayport State University sweatshirt.

Job woes momentarily forgotten, Danielle jumped to her feet, the chair scraping across the linoleum. "Here, have a seat." All the bandages had been removed from Jenny's face, but it was still marred by discoloration. Jenny's hands trembled.

Jenny shrugged her sister off. "You've been treating me like a china doll since I got home from the hospital. I'm fine." She pulled open the refrigerator door, stared at its contents for a moment, then slammed it shut, rattling the glass jars. "What's keeping you here?" Jenny pivoted slowly and leaned back on the door for support. "I'm home. I can take care of Gram." She was clearly irritated. "You're free to go." She rolled her eyes. "You can't babysit me forever."

Danielle tipped her head from side to side, trying to work out the kinks in her neck. She decided to ignore her sister's comments and she sat back down. Something else about her sister was weighing on her mind. "You got a message on your phone last night."

"My phone?" The color drained from Jenny's already pale face. "The police gave you my phone?"

"Yesterday." Danielle angled her head to study her little sister. "You don't remember leaving it at home before you went out the night of your accident?"

Jenny cocked an eyebrow and shook her head. Playing with the ends of the drawstring on her sweatshirt, she finally said, "Aren't you going to give me the phone?"

"I don't have it. I gave it to Patrick."

Jenny narrowed her gaze. "Are you going to tell me what the text said?"

"B needed you to make a delivery." Danielle crossed her arms and rested them on the table.

Jenny collapsed into the chair. She tipped her head back and briefly closed her eyes. "This is a nightmare."

Danielle slid her hand across the table, her fingers brushing the back of Jenny's hand. "Please tell me what you're caught up in."

A hurt look descended into her little sister's eyes. The same look she used to get when their mother announced they were moving, yet again. "I made one mistake. I took some pills Henry gave me. I am not, nor was I ever a dealer. I have no idea what that message was all about."

Relief washed over Danielle. She couldn't exactly explain why, but she believed her sister on her word alone. The open, honest look on Jenny's face said it all. Patting her hand, she said, "I believe you and I'm sorry you got caught up in this. I will do whatever I can to help you."

A small smile played at the corners of Jenny's mouth. Tears gathered in her eyes. "Thank you. But it's time for you to go back to Atlanta. If you lose your job—" she laughed, "—I've got enough guilt already."

Danielle squeezed her hand. "Please don't worry. I'll be fine."

A soft shuffling came from the stairs. Gram appeared at the archway in her Sunday best. "Get ready for church. Patrick is going to pick us up in thirty minutes."

Danielle opened her mouth to protest when Gram put her hand up. "I won't take no for an answer. We have much to be thankful for."

Patrick's rich baritone voice drifted over to Danielle as she sat two seats away in the small congregation. She had forgotten how much she enjoyed these church hymns. How they filled her heart. When she glanced across to Patrick—over Ava's head—he stared straight ahead, but a wry smile graced his lips. Had he heard her humming along?

When the song finished, he leaned over. "Are you enjoying the service?" he asked in a soft whisper.

She tipped her head, unwilling to answer while in the house of God. But she did feel a certain peace, something she hadn't felt in a long time. When she allowed herself to scan the congregation, she noticed a few of the women openly staring at her with interest. Smiling to herself, she knew she and Patrick, with a beaming Ava between them, looked like the happy family. If only they knew.

From where she sat, Danielle noticed Chief Parker and Jimmy. The chief had his uniform on and Jimmy had on a shirt and tie, something few young adults did in church anymore. "There's Jimmy," Danielle whispered in her sister's ear.

Jenny didn't bother looking around, but her knuckles grew white as she gripped the bench in front of her. "Are you okay?"

Jenny nodded, but didn't lift her eyes. Danielle glanced over to where Jimmy stood and found him staring at her. A chill raced down her spine.

When the church service was over, they all filed out. As they milled around the lobby, chatting with other members of the congregation, Danielle feigned interest in a wall of brochures while standing within earshot of Jimmy and Jenny.

"Come on, babe," Jimmy said in a soft tone. "I miss you."

Jenny dragged a shaky hand through her hair. "I need some time to figure things out."

Yes! Danielle did a subtle fist pump before turning away to hide the smile on her face.

"It's not because..." Jimmy's voice trailed off, making it impossible for Danielle to hear him.

"Everything's fine. Just give me some time," Jenny said to her boyfriend.

"Find anything interesting?" Patrick walked up, a huge smile on his handsome face.

"I'm starving. Can we grab some donuts on the way home?"

He chuckled. "Let's round up the troops."

Just then, Chief Parker made his way over to them. "I have some news, Patrick."

"I'll wait by the door," Danielle said, sensing the two police officers needed to talk in private.

He shook his head. "This will interest you. We arrested Billy last night. He had a sizeable amount of drugs in his trunk." Chief Parker's steady gaze landed squarely on Danielle. "I think you and your sister can sleep better tonight."

"You cold?" Patrick asked after noticing Danielle pull her fleece coat closed. He draped his arm over the back of the park bench, inches from Danielle's shoulder. They'd driven to the lake after taking everyone home from church. With Billy's surprise arrest, the crisis in Mayport seemed to be winding down. Danielle would be going home soon, and he didn't want their relationship to end. Not like it had last time.

"A little." Shrugging, she leaned into him. He tucked a strand of her shiny auburn hair behind her ear. It seemed like the most natural thing to do.

He gestured toward the dock with his chin. "Hey, I have the keys to the police boat. Want to take it out?"

Danielle gave him a sideways look. "I'm not exactly dressed for an outing on the lake." She smiled. "Who knew your boating skills would become a professional asset."

"Go figure. I love boating. Just wish the season were longer."

"True." She stared over the water, seemingly distracted.

"Is the law firm putting pressure on you to return?" Patrick asked.

Danielle drew in a deep breath, her warm body leaning against his. He wondered if this is all they'd ever have. A few stolen kisses. A cozy moment on a park bench. He wanted more.

She cleared her throat. "The work at the firm is only part of the reason. I've also been doing some work on the side." She glanced up at him, the sun reflecting in her brilliant blue eyes. "I'm helping a mother and her son who are at risk of losing their house. The law firm doesn't know about it."

Looking away, she continued, "I have to help Tina. I know the pain of not having a home." A tear escaped and ran down her cheek. He reached out and wiped it away. She tipped her head toward his hand. "You should see her little boy. He has these big brown eyes." She shook her head. "I can't let them down."

Patrick squeezed her hand. "You're doing a good thing."

Danielle gave her head a quick shake. "I read about her plight in the newspaper and felt compelled to help."

"Have you ever thought of working with families in Mayport?" Patrick moved his thumb back and forth across the back of her hand. "Atlanta doesn't have the lock on families facing foreclosure."

Swiping the back of her hand across her wet cheek, she shifted away to more fully face him. He immediately missed the warmth of her body. "Unfortunately, helping Tina comes from the heart. The clients from the law firm pay the bills." Her pink lips curved into a sad smile. "It's a nice dream though."

"It doesn't have to be a dream. If you moved back to Mayport, it would give us a chance to get to know each other again." Patrick angled his head to look into her eyes. He had a tough time reading what was going on in there.

Danielle waved her hand and briefly closed her eyes. "I like you, Patrick. I really do. But you have a daughter and I'm not mother material. I proved that at the fall festival."

His heart squeezed at the pain evident on her face. "I've always been protective of Ava. She's my only daughter. Being in law enforcement makes me more aware of all the creeps out there." He shook his head. "You didn't know."

"I should have known not to let her go off with her friends." She let out a nervous laugh. "It's all a dream. Working with the clients I want to work with." She lowered her gaze. "Getting to know you again." She shrugged. "I've worked too hard to get where I am." She paused. "I'm not willing to give up the security."

"Money isn't the only means of security," Patrick said, already seeing her slip away.

"Easy for you to say. You've always had money. A home…"

Patrick reached out and grabbed her hands in his. "Don't run away. Stay—"

Danielle's cell phone rang, cutting him off midsentence. Patrick leaned back, disappointed. He didn't want to compete with a cell phone. What he had to say was too important. She lifted an eyebrow as if to apologize. She plucked the cell phone from her purse and glanced down at the display. Splotches of red fired in her cheeks.

"Hello." Her voice sounded shaky. After a pause, she added, "I don't know. No, I'm with Officer Kingsley." She jumped to her feet and gestured to Patrick. "We'll check it out now."

Danielle snapped the phone shut, her eyes wide with alarm. "Something triggered the alarm at home. Gram's visiting with a friend. Jenny's alone and she's not answering the alarm company's call."

Patrick called into the station as they raced to the house. As he pulled up the rutted driveway, nothing seemed out of place. He jammed the gearshift into park and turned to

Danielle, who was sitting ramrod straight in the passenger seat. "Stay here while I check it out."

Patrick found the side door ajar. The muffled sounds of the strident alarm horn blared through the walls. Long gone were the days when people mounted outside horns annoying the neighbors with false alarms. Instead, they were mounted in basements, their ear-piercing noise a treat for burglars and homeowners who unwittingly tripped the device. With his hand hovering over his gun, he pushed the door open. He stepped into the kitchen where he was met with an apologetic Henry.

"I tried every number combination possible, but I can't shut the dumb thing up."

"Where's Jenny?" Patrick asked.

"Locked in the upstairs bathroom. She won't come out." Henry dragged a hand through his mussed hair. "I'm really sorry."

Danielle poked her head inside the door. When she saw it was Henry, she stepped in and planted her fists on her hips. "What are you doing here?"

He jabbed his thumb toward his toolbox. "I have the part I need to finish the work on the upstairs bathroom."

"I don't want you here when I'm not here." Danielle's harsh words competed with the deafening sound of the alarm.

Henry tipped his head and lifted a brow. "Think you can take care of that before I go deaf?"

Danielle narrowed her gaze at Henry. "Turn around." When he did, she punched in the code, and the kitchen fell quiet. She spun around. "Where's Jenny?"

"She won't come out of the bathroom. I think the alarm freaked her out."

"You stay here." Danielle gave Henry a pointed stare.

Patrick picked up the rusted, red toolbox, was surprised by its weight and handed it to Henry. "You'll have to finish the job another day. But make sure you clear it first, okay?"

Henry nodded. Worry seemed to widen his eyes. "I'm not going to lose my job over this, am I? I really need the money for school."

"Just let it blow over. Go on now." Patrick tipped his head toward the door. Henry started to walk out and Patrick called him back. "Is there anything else you'd like to tell me?"

Henry shook his head. "No, sir."

"I've heard some disturbing information about you." Henry's eyes flared wide. "I'll be looking into it." Patrick pointed at Henry's chest. "Word to the wise, keep your nose clean."

"Yes, sir, but I had nothing to do with Jenny's accident."

Patrick's intuition perked up and his eyes narrowed. "Never said you did. But know this, we're watching you."

"No need, sir." Henry backed toward the door.

"Let me be the judge." Patrick watched Henry as he left, wondering if the kid with the stricken expression on his face was capable of beating a woman. Sometimes he hated this job. He turned and ran upstairs. He found Danielle standing in the bathroom doorway. Jenny sat in the empty bathtub, her legs pulled up to her chest, her face buried in her knees.

"How'd you open the door?"

Danielle lifted a bobby pin pinched between her fingers. "She won't talk to me."

Patrick pushed into the room and sat down on the edge of the tub. "Jenny?"

Jenny blinked back tears. Her entire body shook with sobs. "I thought he was coming for me."

Patrick locked gazes with Danielle. She frowned and lifted

her palms. He placed a comforting hand on Jenny's shoulder. "Who was coming for you?"

Jenny shook her head. She batted away his hand, then planted her palms on the edge of the tub and pulled herself up. She stepped over the edge of the tub and marched out of the bathroom.

Danielle caught her arm. "Tell us what you know."

Jenny pulled away, her expression pinched. "I—" she shook her head as if clearing the image, "—the alarm freaked me out. That's all." She dropped down onto the bed.

"You're not telling me something," Danielle said in a gentle voice. "Please, please tell me who hurt you." She sat next to her sister, yet seemed unsure of what to do with her hands. The scene tore at Patrick's heart.

"You need to tell us. Was it Billy? Someone who worked for Billy? We can protect you," Patrick said, crouching down in front of Jenny. The alarm had triggered some sort of flashback for Jenny. Had someone come into her home the night of her accident? Pulled her from her bed? He was convinced now more than ever that Jenny was hiding something. Maybe she hadn't forgotten.

Jenny's steely eyes telegraphed what was etched in his heart. *You already failed me.*

Chapter Fifteen

Danielle plopped down on her childhood bed and ran her hand across the worn comforter. It had been exactly two weeks since her frantic trip home after Jenny's accident. And now, with Billy Farr in custody and her sister on the mend, she planned to return to Atlanta in the morning. So why did she feel so blah? Perhaps because she worried about her sister's psyche. Jenny wasn't talking much about the attack, but was doing her best to convince everyone she was fine, and it was time to get on with things.

It also didn't help that Danielle had to return to her job, knowing she'd have to work like a dog to get herself back into the good graces of the partners of the law firm. She stuffed a shirt into her suitcase and wondered if she had completely derailed her career, everything she had worked for.

Danielle rolled her shoulders and drew in a deep breath. She had spent the better part of the last week lining up repairmen to make repairs on the house because she refused to allow Henry back into Gram's home. She'd discussed long-term plans with her sister on how they could keep Gram in the house. And she spent some time with Patrick, but had made it abundantly clear that neither Mayport nor he was in her future. All in all, she'd had a busy week.

Danielle pulled another shirt off the wire hanger in the

closet and pressed it close to her chest. Maybe that's why she couldn't shake this gloom. Was she too willing to walk away from a second chance with Patrick? She flung the shirt into the open suitcase. No, she had worked too hard to just throw away her career. Her mother had walked away from her children for a man. She refused to give up her independence. Her security.

But Patrick isn't any man...

Over the course of the week, she'd found herself reflecting in prayer. But myriad worries barraged her brain, never allowing her to be still long enough to listen. Maybe she wasn't wired for prayer. She had to make a decision based on facts. And the fact was she liked having money and security.

The doorbell sounded downstairs, startling Danielle. Butterflies fluttered in her stomach. Could it be Patrick? He had to know she was leaving tomorrow morning. She smoothed a hand over her hair and pinched her cheeks for color. She ran downstairs and opened the front door. Ava. Her heart squeezed. Danielle would really miss this little girl. Ava bounced on the balls of her feet as if she had a secret.

"Well, hello there, Ava." The pair had grown very close. Ava had stopped by after school every day this week. Danielle tried to be the type of adult she wished she'd had in her life when she was ten. Each time she saw the child's smiling face, a tiny part of her heart ached. The more attached she grew, the harder it would be to leave. She had to leave. Soon. Hanging around wasn't fair to anyone. Least of all to this beautiful little girl.

"I have this for you." Ava offered Danielle a shocking-pink envelope.

Danielle slipped her finger under the flap and eased a piece of dark purple construction paper from the envelope. Colorful butterflies flittered across the page. "This is beautiful. Did you make it?"

"Yeah." Ava smiled shyly. "It's an invitation. I wanted to have you over for dinner before you left." The little girl pushed out her lower lip and Danielle detected a slight tremble. "Do you really have to go?"

Danielle tipped her head and studied the child. Tears burned the backs of her eyes. Fearing she'd collapse in a blubbering heap, she gazed over Ava's head to the stately white home across the lawn. The home that represented everything she'd never have.

"Are you okay, Miss Danielle? You look sad." Ava's small hand slipped into Danielle's. A yearning she never knew she had tugged at her heart. "Or are those happy tears?"

Danielle drew in a deep breath, then exhaled. She bent over and kissed the top of Ava's head. "They're happy tears."

"Good, so you'll come?" An eager expression lit Ava's face.

"Does Bunny know about this?" She thought back to the uncomfortable Sunday dinner nearly two weeks ago. Had it really been only two weeks ago?

Ava's green eyes widened and she nodded vigorously. "My dad knows too."

Danielle looked down at the handcrafted invitation and her heart swelled. How could she say no to this beautiful child? "I'd be happy to come. What can I bring?"

"Bunny said to just bring yourself." Ava turned and bounded down the porch steps with a spring in her step. She stopped and spun back around. "Oh, and make sure Gram and Jenny come with you."

With Ava's invitation in hand, Danielle went into the living room. Gram had an expectant look on her face. Her pale brows furrowed. "Why the long face? Sounds like we have a nice dinner invitation."

"It's not that...I'm tired."

Gram reached out for Danielle's hand. Danielle lowered herself onto the footstool in front of her grandmother. "You must be exhausted. I'm grateful you were able to get away from work and come home."

Home. The word still had a distant ring to it. Was Mayport home? Or Atlanta? Her head swirled with too many disjointed thoughts. She lifted Gram's hand and kissed the soft skin.

Gram cupped Danielle's chin with her warm palm. "Did you ever think about staying?"

Danielle laughed, then sobered. "Here? In Mayport?"

A small smile pulled at Gram's lips, softening the lines around her mouth. "You could be happy here."

"Maybe. But I've worked hard. I could be a partner soon. And with this economy, I'm lucky to have a job."

"You can always find excuses if you're looking for them." Gram fingered the red ribbon marking the page in her Bible sitting open on her lap. "And that sweet child looks up to you."

Danielle bit her lower lip, trying to keep it from shaking. "She is sweet."

"And what about Patrick?" Gram asked when the silence stretched between them.

"Patrick?" Danielle asked coyly as she shifted on the corner of the footstool.

"Oh, don't give me that."

Danielle shook her head.

"You used to be such good friends."

"That was a long time ago." Back then, Danielle was naive. She had nothing to lose.

"Two people don't often get a second chance." *Second*

chance. There were those words again. "God works in mysterious ways."

She didn't know much about that, but she had too much respect for her grandmother to say differently.

"I see the way you look at him," Gram said.

Heat crept up Danielle's face.

"Oh, don't be getting shy with me. I remember how you used to pine after him, staring like a lovesick child across the lawn."

"Don't remind me. I was a fool."

"No such thing. Don't you think I see how he looks at you?"

Danielle narrowed her gaze, hope blossoming in her chest. She saw it too, but hearing her grandmother say it made it more real. "You're a hopeless romantic, Gram."

Gram ran a strand of Danielle's hair through her fingers. "For such a sophisticated big-city girl, you sure miss the obvious. Don't let your mother's sins ruin your life."

A tear escaped down Danielle's cheek. She quickly wiped it away. Leaning forward, she kissed Gram's soft cheek. "I love you, Gram."

Patrick watched as Ava skipped across the back lawn, her blonde curls bouncing in her excitement over what was sure to be the last picnic of the season. She held something in her hands. "Miss Danielle brought an apple pie."

Patrick clipped the plastic cloth onto the picnic table to prevent it from blowing away. He turned to see Danielle making her way across the lawn, her paced slow as she helped Gram navigate the uneven terrain. His heart tightened. He had hoped he'd be able to convince her to stay.

"I made an apple pie," Bunny muttered under her breath as she glanced at the one Danielle had sent over. "Quick, Patrick, take mine and put it in the fridge. We'll serve hers."

"Thanks, Mom."

Bunny smiled, softer than usual, and planted a kiss on her son's cheek. "Danielle is our guest."

Patrick narrowed his gaze. "Does this have anything to do with the fact that she's leaving tomorrow?"

A light twinkled in Bunny's eyes. She shook her head. "No. Actually, for Ava's sake, I'm disappointed she's leaving. That child has taken on a new glow." Bunny shrugged. "I think I may have judged Danielle too harshly." She patted Patrick's cheek. "Now go take my pie inside before she sees it."

On his way back out of the house to the grill, Patrick greeted his guests while juggling a plate full of meat. Bunny settled Gram and Jenny on the back porch. Out of the corner of his eye, Patrick saw Danielle making her way to him. She lifted her face to the sun and briefly closed her eyes. "It's a glorious day. Too bad the winter comes so early here."

"The winters are a little easier down south."

Danielle glanced at him with a measured stare. "True. The fall stretches well into December."

"And not much snow."

"No, but when it does snow, it's usually the big wet flakes." Tiny lines formed around her twinkling blue eyes. "And it's crazy. When it snows down there, people use umbrellas. Can you imagine?"

He shook his head and watched her hands flutter when she talked. She was beautiful, but he couldn't help but lament they had resorted to talking about the weather.

"I'm glad you made it for dinner."

"I could never say no to Ava." Her gaze drifted over to his daughter who was taking drink orders from her guests. "She's quite the hostess."

"She takes after her mother."

Their eyes met and locked—perhaps it had been the mention of Lisa. Maybe his deceased wife was part of the reason Danielle refused to give them a chance. Did Danielle doubt he had room in his heart for her too? He opened his mouth to say something—perhaps this would be his last chance before she left—when Ava came skipping over.

"Want some lemonade, Miss Danielle? I made it myself. Or," she added with less enthusiasm, "we have bottled water."

"Lemonade sounds great."

"Okay." Ava smiled brightly before skipping toward the house.

The sun glinted off something gold around Danielle's elegant neck. Curious, Patrick reached out and took the liberty of brushing his finger against her warm neck, then under the chain. An audible gasp escaped her lips. "May I?" He didn't wait for an answer. Gently, he tugged at the chain until he exposed the gold cross hidden under her clothing. He pinched the cross between his fingers and placed it on top of her sweater, the gold color prominent against the blue material.

Danielle flattened her hand on top of the cross, as if she had only now realized she had it on. "Gram found it in her jewelry box. It was mine from when I made my confirmation." She shrugged. "I guess I left it behind when I went away to college."

"And you're wearing it now..." Patrick let his words trail off, not wanting to make any assumptions. But he couldn't deny the hope filling his heart.

"My grandmother means the world to me. It makes her

happy." Danielle's checks grew flushed.

"Patrick, I could use a hand," Bunny hollered from the back door.

"Can we talk later?" Patrick asked, disappointed that their conversation had been interrupted.

"Sure. Let's go help Bunny."

Danielle drank in the moment, memorizing every detail to savor at a later date. From the way Ava's eyes sparkled as she talked about her latest knitting project, to the content look on Gram's face, to the spectacular display of color God had painted in the leaves. She paused for a moment. Had she really thought in terms of God? She lifted her fingers to the gold cross and then quickly dropped her hand. Maybe it wasn't too late to teach an old dog new tricks. Smiling, she turned and found Patrick studying her from across the picnic table. Her cheeks grew warm. The hole in her heart seemed to grow smaller.

Doubt crept into her mind.

"Do you like the salad, Miss Danielle?" Ava asked. She stabbed a grape tomato and lifted it on her fork. "I made it."

"It's delicious."

Ava popped the tomato into her mouth and chewed it thoughtfully. "Are you going to come back and visit us soon?"

Danielle felt a bittersweet tug at her heart. She quickly glanced around the table. Everyone seemed focused on their meals. Danielle forced a smile. "Ava, I'll come back and visit."

"You promise?" The little girl stared at her intently with those green eyes reminiscent of Patrick's.

"I promise I will come back to visit more often."

"As long as she doesn't forget about us once she's back at

her fancy law firm." Leaning on the picnic table, Jenny pushed herself to a standing position, a smile playing on her lips, and she winked. She pulled one leg, then the other, over the picnic bench. Over the past week, Danielle had seemed to mend the fence with her sister, and she was especially pleased when Jenny'd announced she and Jimmy were taking a break, at least until she figured out what she wanted from life. Jimmy had been persistent with his phone calls, but Jenny'd seemed more determined with each day. Danielle was proud of her.

Gram's eyes slid to Patrick. "Oh, I think she'll be coming around a little more."

Jenny picked up her plate and glass. "I think it's great Danielle's going back to Atlanta. It seems to suit her."

Despite all their heart-to-hearts this week, Jenny had been adamant that Danielle leave Mayport. She felt a twinge of disappointment. Why didn't Jenny want her to stick around?

"Thanks for dinner," Jenny said, pulling the collar up on her jacket. "Can I help carry anything in before I go?"

"Are you sure you won't stay for dessert?" Bunny asked.

Jenny waved her hand. "No, thank you. I'm tired."

Patrick stood and offered his arm. "Let me walk you home."

A tired smile turned up the corners of Jenny's lips. "No, I'm good. Please, sit down. Enjoy the company." With rounded shoulders, Jenny turned and walked away.

Danielle forced a smile. Pivoting on the end of the bench, she rose to her feet. "Thank you for dinner. It was a lovely evening. I probably should be going too." She reached over and picked up her plate. "I have to finish packing. Gram, are you ready to go?"

"I can walk Gram home in a little bit. We haven't even had dessert." Danielle didn't miss the disappointment in Ava's voice.

"Thanks, sweetheart. That would be wonderful."

A shrill cry came from around the front of the house. The fine hairs on the back of Danielle's neck stood at attention. *Jenny.* She dropped her plate and glass on the table and ran in the direction of her sister's cry.

"Let me go," Jenny cried, her fisted hands protected her scrunched-up face.

"You're lying. You're lying. You have to tell the truth. " Debbie, Billy Farr's girlfriend, had Jenny by the shoulders, shaking her, forcing her head to bob back and forth.

"Stop!" Patrick yelled as he ran past Danielle. He grabbed ahold of Debbie and pried her fingers from Jenny, who was clearly shaken. He pulled Debbie's arms behind her back. The crazed look in her eyes sent a chill down Danielle's spine.

"Billy did not hurt you. And he's not a drug dealer. Someone set him up. Someone put those drugs in his trunk." Debbie's voice rose to a higher and higher decibel, piercing Danielle's eardrums. A small child's wailing floated up from the rusted-out car idling in the driveway. "He wouldn't do drugs. We have a child. You have to tell the truth."

Danielle drew Jenny into a protective embrace. Her sister's lips trembled and what little color she had drained from her face. Shoulders trembling, Jenny bowed her head and hid her face in her hands.

"Debbie," Patrick said, his voice compassionate, "you need to pull yourself together. For your daughter's sake."

A *whoop, whoop* of a siren sounded from the end of the drive. Chief Parker raced up the driveway, his vehicle chewing up gravel. He pushed open his door and strode toward them, his hand hovering over his gun. "What's going on out here?" He gestured with his chin toward Jenny. "Is she hurt?"

Jenny lowered her hands and shook her head. "No, she

183

didn't hurt me. I'm fine."

"Who called you, Chief?" Patrick asked.

Ava poked her head out the front door, phone in hand. The fear on Ava's face made Danielle's stomach drop. She had seen that look many times before on her little sister's face when their mother yelled at them in a drunken rage. She shook the thought away. Her fried nerves couldn't deal right now.

"I ran into the house." Ava'd finally found her voice. "I heard Miss Debbie yelling. I was scared. You always told me to call 9-1-1 in an emergency."

Patrick met his daughter on the front porch. Ava wrapped her arms around his waist and buried her head. He smoothed a hand down her curls. "You did the right thing. I'm proud of you. Go inside. I'll be in shortly." He gave her a kiss, then opened the front door. Bunny took her granddaughter's hand.

Chief Parker unhooked the handcuffs from his utility belt. "What's going on here?"

Debbie tilted her chin in Jenny's direction. "She's lying about Billy. Now the father of my baby is in prison. How am I supposed to keep a roof over our heads?"

Chief Parker approached Patrick. "What do you want to do here? I could take her in for trespassing." He narrowed his gaze at Jenny. "Assault?"

Jenny pulled away from Danielle, crouched down and hugged her legs to her body. She buried her face in her knees. Rocking back and forth on her heels, her body shook with sobs. Danielle knelt beside Jenny and pulled her into an embrace. Jenny shrugged off Danielle's arm.

"Are you okay, Jenny?" Patrick asked.

Jenny lifted her face, revealing wet cheeks. "Yes. Please just make her leave." She hiccupped over a sob. "Let her go home with her baby."

Chief Parker nodded. He took Debbie by the arm and led her to the car. He talked to her in a low voice before yanking open the car door for her. She grabbed the door frame, refusing to get in. Wrenching free from Chief Parker's grasp, she opened the back door and unbuckled her child from the car seat.

The child's wails subsided into muffled whimpering as she tucked her face into the crook of her mother's neck. Debbie marched over to Jenny and hovered over her, her menacing expression softened by the child in her arms.

Debbie smoothed a hand down her daughter's hair, a pleading look in her eyes. "Please do the right thing. For my little girl." The hard anger on Debbie's face crumbled into something completely different—fear, grief, a profound sadness.

Jenny pressed a hand to her mouth, but didn't say anything.

"Debbie, please," Danielle said, her heart breaking into a million pieces, "don't do this. Billy is dangerous. Maybe it's better this way. You won't be raising a child in the same house as a—"

"Shut up," Debbie said, the cords in her neck growing taut, "just shut up. Billy is my daughter's father. He'd never do anything to hurt us." The woman lifted her chin in a defiant gesture. "Your little sister ain't so innocent either. Billy told me she was trying to buy drugs the other night. For all I know she planted those drugs. Set him up to save her butt."

Patrick was at their sides in a heartbeat. "Debbie, it's time you left. Take your little girl home. She needs you."

He reached out to take her arm, but she jerked away. "I don't need your help." She swung around and glowered in Jenny's direction. "I need *her* to tell the truth."

Danielle wrapped her arm around Jenny's trembling frame

and drew her to a standing position. "Are you okay?"

Jenny bowed her head and took a deep breath.

"You have to stay strong," Chief Parker said. "These people have a way of whining and manipulating things until they get their way. We found drugs in his possession. That's what got her boyfriend locked up. Not you. Stay strong. Her baby will be better off out from under the same roof as that no-good drug dealer."

"Where will they go?" Jenny asked, her voice shaking. "Where will they go if they can't afford the house?"

Danielle pushed a strand of Jenny's hair behind her ear. "Jenny, Chief Parker's right. You're doing the right thing. It's not your fault Billy's a dealer. They need to keep him off the street so he doesn't hurt anyone else." She squeezed her sister's shoulders, trying to infuse her with strength, relieved her sister didn't push her away.

"Listen to your sister here." Chief Parker tipped his hat then turned to leave. The group seemed transfixed—shocked maybe—as they watched the police cruiser pull away.

When his taillights had disappeared down the street, Ava ran out the front door and across the yard. She clung to her father's hand. "Did I do the right thing calling the police?"

"Of course, sweetheart. Sometimes even the police—" he pointed to his chest, "—need back up." He smoothed a hand down her hair. "Why don't you run inside and brush your teeth. Get ready for bed. I'll be there in a minute."

"I'll take Jenny and Gram home and get them some tea to calm their nerves," Bunny said. The women seemed eager to get out of the chilly night air.

Ava started to go in, then turned back around. "Will I see you tomorrow?" she asked Danielle, a longing look in her eyes.

Danielle bent down in front of Ava, her heart breaking. "I have an early flight."

"Oh." Ava lowered her gaze and stuck out her lower lip.

"Miss Danielle has a job she needs to get home to." Patrick playfully shook his daughter's hand. Ava pulled from his grasp and wrapped her arms around Danielle's neck. Danielle froze, not sure what to do.

Then instinct kicked in. She cupped Ava's face between her hands. The little green eyes—just like her father's—were very expressive. "I am very happy I got to know you. You're a great girl."

Ava flashed a huge smile. "Thank you."

"If I don't go back, they might fire me." Danielle suddenly felt she had to justify leaving.

Ava shook her head. "No they wouldn't. You're too nice."

"Being nice has nothing to do with it. You have to do a good job. Like when you're in school. You have to study and work hard to get good grades."

Ava nodded as if she understood. "But if you got fired, you could stay here."

"I need to make money—" she lifted her hand to the house behind her, "—to pay for a place to live, food to eat..." She let her words trail off. How did she explain her lingering insecurity? When Danielle was ten, she never knew if they'd have to leave their apartment in the middle of the night because her mom was behind on the rent. She gently tugged a strand of Ava's hair. "So I have to go."

Ava's eyes brightened. "Stay here with us. You wouldn't need a job."

Danielle spun around to find Patrick watching the exchange, a somber expression on his face. She arched her brows and drew her mouth into a hard line. *I need some help here, Patrick.*

"She could, couldn't she, Dad?" Ava ran over and tugged her father's hand.

Patrick lifted Ava's hand and gave it a kiss. "Sweetheart—" his eyes lingered on Danielle's above his daughter's head, "— Miss Danielle has an important job she has to get back to in Atlanta."

On the surface, his words seemed sincere, but she sensed a tinge of derision, or maybe disappointment. Surely he didn't expect her to give up her job. A battle of words waged in her head. She couldn't give up her job just because her relationship with Patrick *might* develop into something more. She needed more than that.

Ava took Danielle's outstretched hand. "I'll visit soon." She squeezed the little girl's hand as she fought back tears.

"Promise?"

Danielle pressed her lips together and nodded. Leaning over, she kissed the crown of Ava's head. She tapped her gently on the back. "Now listen to your dad. Go get ready for bed."

Ava groaned but did as she was told. Patrick stood rooted in place. The silence stretched between them. "Well." He was the first to speak. "I guess this is goodbye."

Danielle hitched a shoulder as she fought to keep her lower lip from quivering.

"Did you mean what you said?" he asked, stuffing his hands into the front pockets of his jeans.

Danielle's eyes narrowed.

"About coming back to visit more often," Patrick said, ending her confusion.

"Oh." Danielle shrugged. "Of course I'll be back." She

glanced over her shoulder toward Gram's house. "I think Gram and Jenny need some looking after. I don't want this mess to derail my sister's college dreams."

Patrick let out a long breath. "Give her time. I'll keep an eye on them." He tipped his head toward their house. "I'm right here."

She nodded. "That's good to know."

"Dani..." He let her name hang out there. She felt her breath hitch, the air charged with expectation. He stepped closer and tipped her chin to meet his gaze. His warm touch flowed through her entire body. "I hope someday you'll stop living in the past." He brushed his lips across hers and she craved more of his solid nearness. Without meaning to, she pressed against him. He deepened the kiss before pulling away suddenly, leaving her flushed and chilled at the same time. "Night, Danielle. Have a safe trip...home."

Chapter Sixteen

Danielle found Jenny sitting at the kitchen table drinking a cup of tea. "Gram's already in bed," Jenny said, answering her sister's unasked question. She cradled her mug between both hands and blew on the hot liquid. For the briefest of moments, Jenny was a ten-year-old girl drinking hot chocolate in a cold apartment their mother couldn't afford to heat.

Danielle slipped into the seat across from Jenny. "Bunny didn't stay long."

"No. She just made sure we got in all right. Gram was tired—" she lifted the mug to her lips and took a sip, "—and I'm more than capable of making my own hot cocoa."

"Well, it was nice of her to walk you home."

Jenny lifted her brows but didn't say anything.

Her sister was still understandably rattled from the encounter with Billy Farr's girlfriend. "Are you okay?"

"Just dandy." Jenny rolled her eyes.

"Do you think Mom was an evil person?" The question seemed to come out of nowhere.

Danielle closed her eyes briefly, trying to picture their mother's face, her rare smile. "Evil?" She shook her head. "No, I think she was misguided. I think she made a lot of bad decisions. As life went on, she became more reliant on men for basic needs. She forgot what was truly important." She reached across the table and touched her little sister's trembling hands.

"She forgot about us." Jenny's voice sounded soft, almost childlike. She lifted her eyes. "Sometimes I think I know how she felt."

Danielle narrowed her gaze. "What do you mean?" Her stomach tightened.

"I understand what it means to get completely tied up in another person and losing yourself."

Squeezing her sister's hand as if to punctuate her words, Danielle said, "You never have to rely on a man. I can help you until you get on your feet." She studied the top of her sister's bowed head. When Jenny didn't respond, Danielle said, "Promise me you'll come to me first if you need anything."

Jenny lifted her face, tears streaming down her cheeks. "I promise." She wiped her tears on the edge of her sleeve. "Maybe—" she fluttered her hands, "—maybe this whole mess was a blessing in disguise. I was on the wrong path and now I have an opportunity to change." The corners of her mouth curved into a small smile. "I've been doing a lot of praying about it."

Danielle smiled in return. She too had reached out in prayer for guidance but still felt lost. Perhaps her constant worry about her job hadn't allowed room to let God in.

Inwardly, she shook the thought away. "I'm leaving in the morning, but I'll be back soon. And I'm only a phone call away." A lump formed in her throat, making it difficult to speak. "I can't thank you enough for taking care of Gram all these years. I've been selfish."

"Self-preservation." Jenny lifted an eyebrow. "We all did what we had to do."

Self-preservation? Strange choice of words. Is that what

191

Jenny was doing now?

"Are you and Jimmy really over?" Danielle held her breath, waiting for the answer.

Jenny shrugged. "I need to discover myself."

"You'll go back to school, right?" Danielle tried to keep her eagerness in check.

"I hope to." Jenny pushed back her chair and rolled her shoulders. Under the bare light bulb, the flesh under her eyes seemed darker than normal. She planted her palms on the table and bent down to look into Danielle's eyes. "I'm not Mom. And—" she pulled back into an upright position, "—and neither are you."

"I never..." Danielle let her words trail off, hating the shaky sound of her voice.

"I know. I know." Jenny's words flowed out on a tired sigh. "I know you look at me and think I have so much to accomplish. And trust me, I do. But you're so afraid of not having a good job and security that you're missing out on everything else." She tapped her fingers on the table. "You think you have it all, but you don't." Jenny put her mug in the sink, then crossed to Danielle and kissed her cheek. "I love you, big sister."

The tiny kitchen made Danielle feel claustrophobic. She pulled her jacket off the hook by the door and flipped on the light switch, illuminating the twinkling strands adorning the gazebo. The fragrant smell of autumn wafted to her nose as she kicked the dried leaves. She glanced toward the Kingsley's home. It seemed like a lifetime ago that she and Ava had bonded over jumping in leaves. It all felt like a dream.

She ran her hand along the wood of the gazebo, then dropped into Gram's rocker. She tipped her head back and stared at the clouds as they floated past the moon. The stars were out in full force tonight. If she racked her brain, she could probably name a handful of constellations. Too tired, she let her thoughts drift. She'd miss this when she got back home. It never got dark enough in midtown Atlanta to enjoy the full display of God's handiwork.

God's handiwork. She let her eyes drift closed, the soft breeze caressing her cheeks, trying to memorize this day. This moment.

From a distance, she heard leaves crunching, the sound of feet moving quickly across the yard. She straightened her back, every nerve ending buzzing. A small shadow appeared under the light by the back door.

"Ava!" Danielle stood.

The little girl glanced over her shoulder. A smile brightened her face when she saw Danielle standing by the gazebo. She took off in a full sprint and wrapped her arms around Danielle's waist in a fierce hug and buried her face. "You can't leave. I'll miss you too much."

Danielle dragged her hand down the girl's downy hair, tears burning the backs of her eyes. "You shouldn't be out here. Your father will be worried."

Ava's tiny frame racked with sobs.

"Please don't cry, sweetie. I'll be back." Her heart broke for the child.

Ava looked up, tears glistening in her eyes. "I want you to live here."

Danielle ran a finger across Ava's wet cheek. "You're going to make me cry." Her voice shook. "And not happy tears." She tried to lighten the mood. "Let me walk you home before your dad sends out a search party." She clasped Ava's tiny hand and stepped off the gazebo.

The sound of glass shattering made her stop. She drew Ava protectively behind her. Ice shot through her veins and her pulse quickened.

"What was that noise?" Ava asked, her voice trembling.

Danielle glanced toward the noise, toward the house. "I don't—"

A huge explosion sounded from the front of the house. An orange fireball lit the night. Danielle's heart dropped. "Gram! Jenny!" She crouched down, her face inches from Ava's. "Run home. Get your dad."

Ava froze. Danielle nudged her shoulder. "Run. Now."

The little girl took off toward her house. Danielle ran to the side door and yanked it open. A calloused hand came down hard over her mouth and lifted her off her feet. A crushing blow to the side of her head sent an explosion of pain shooting through her skull.

Feeling woozy, she feared for Jenny's safety. She reached back and clawed at the man's head. He swore under his breath and punched her head again. Horrified, she couldn't catch her breath.

Darkness claimed her.

Chapter Seventeen

Patrick shot out of bed, stuffing his arms into his flannel shirt as he bolted down the stairs. An explosion had sounded from somewhere close. Dani's house. His pulse roared in his ears. He ran onto the front lawn and heard the panicked cries of his daughter. He crouched down and gripped Ava's forearms. "What are you doing outside?"

Ava trembled under his touch. "Miss Danielle..." She pointed toward the Carson's house. Flames shot from the front window. Terror seized his heart.

"Patrick?" Bunny stood in the doorway, clutching her robe at the collar.

Patrick pointed frantically at her. "Take Ava inside. Call 9-1-1. Stay in the house. Away from the windows. Lock the doors."

"Patrick?" Bunny's eyes shone with fear.

"Now," he demanded. "Do it now."

Bunny pressed her hand to her chest and scurried back into the house, clutching Ava's hand. Assured his family was securely inside, he ran toward the fire. Squinting against the orange-and-red glow of flames, his mind filled with thoughts of Danielle. A thin sheen of sweat slicked his forehead as the panic and heat swarmed around him.

From Danielle's front yard, he saw the entryway engulfed in flames. He ran around the side of the house and found the door yawning open beyond the screen door. Hope bled through him. Maybe they'd already gotten out. He scanned the deep shadows of the darkened yard. "Danielle! Gram! Jenny!"

He waited, his chest heaving. No answer. No one in sight. He grabbed the door handle and the ground beneath him shifted.

Lifting a corner of his flannel shirt to cover his mouth, he pulled open the screen door and pushed inside. Thick smoke rolled through the kitchen. A muffled coughing sounded nearby. He moved deeper into the kitchen. Jenny had her arm wrapped around Gram's waist. "Help," Jenny coughed out.

Patrick slipped his arm around Gram's waist. Her head lolled against his chest. He glanced over his shoulder to make sure Jenny was following, his eyes searching the smoky haze for any sign of Danielle. Panic tightened his gut. "Where's Danielle?"

Jenny coughed in her sleeve, her eyes wide with fear. She shook her head. "I don't know."

The house moaned and creaked under the intense flames. With one arm firmly around Gram's waist, he grabbed Jenny's elbow with his free hand. "Let's get you out of here."

Once he had Gram and Jenny safely outside, Patrick glanced toward the house. Sirens sounded in the distance. Jenny bounced on the balls of her feet, rubbing her hands up and down her bare arms. He sat Gram down on the dewy lawn and patted her hand. "You're going to be okay. The paramedics are on the way. I'm going to get Danielle."

Gram's blue eyes widened. Soot marred her nose and mouth. "Help her," she rasped.

Patrick turned to Jenny. "Where is Danielle?"

Jenny shook her head, tears making tracks down her dirty cheeks. "I ran to her bedroom. Her bed was empty. She wasn't upstairs." A shudder coursed through her body.

Patrick's mind raced with the possibilities. "Where did you last see her?"

"In the kitchen."

A second explosion sounded, sending Patrick and Jenny reeling back. He landed hard on his backside. Jenny landed next to him with a solid thump.

"You okay?" he asked.

Jenny groaned, her wide eyes reflected the brilliant flames consuming the house. "Find Danielle."

A fire truck rumbled up the driveway. A firefighter in full gear jumped off the engine before it came to a complete stop and ran toward them. "Is anyone in the house?"

Patrick pushed past him. "Yes, a woman is in there. Danielle is in there."

The firefighter blocked him. "You can't go in there, sir. It's not safe. Let us handle it."

"I need to find her." Patrick tried to push past the firefighter. Pure adrenaline fueled his forward motion, despite the scorching heat of the flames beating him back.

"Sir, you need to stay out here." The firefighter grabbed Patrick's arm and pulled him back. "I can't let you go in there. And the more you fight me on this, the more time you're wasting."

Patrick's shoulders slumped. He nodded to the firefighter and bowed his head. Bending at the waist, he drew in a shaky breath. His jittery legs gave way and he dropped to his knees.

Dear Lord, please keep Danielle safe. Guide the firefighters to her and bring her out safely.

197

Danielle's mouth felt parched. The hard floor under her swayed. She lifted a hand to her pounding head. Her mind swirled with myriad clips, memories. The explosion. The fire. The calloused hand pressing her upper lip to her teeth. She ran a finger against her swollen lip.

Then darkness.

The haziness began to drift away. The flames. Her family. Danielle stifled a sob and pushed up on her elbow. Pain shot through her head. A wave of nausea rolled over her. She blinked her eyes and barely made out the shapes in the dark.

The scent of algae reached her nose. A subtle *ding, ding* floated in from the not-too-far distance. The rocking motion. Why was she on a boat? Maneuvering to her knees, she swallowed back the nausea and rubbed her pounding head. Getting her bearings, she pushed to her feet and stalked toward the door. Moonlight streamed in through a narrow window. She held her breath as she wrapped her fingers around the door handle. Her heartbeat in her ears was deafening. Locked. The door was locked. Her eyes scanned the room. No other way out.

She rested her back against the door and slid down. Threading her fingers through her hair, she tipped her face upward and pressed her eyes closed. *Dear Lord, I know I haven't exactly made You a part of my life. But I need You. Please, please, please, I beg You. Please let Ava, Jenny and Gram be okay.* She gave her head a quick shake to dismiss the image of the fire, then immediately regretted it. Her nausea welled up. *I haven't always shown it, but I love my family. I need them.* She squeezed her hands together. *And I need You. Please help me.*

From across the room, a shadow moaned, a deep, gruff moan that vibrated through her. She pushed her feet against the floor but failed to gain traction. Her pulse roared in her head. She had nowhere to go.

Her fear morphed into concern. Was someone else hurt? "Who's there?" she whispered.

A male voice cursed. "What the...I'm going to kill that..." He muttered something she couldn't quite hear. The figure seemed to be struggling.

The faint familiarity of the voice seeped into her brain. "Billy? Billy Farr?"

"It ain't the Easter Bunny."

She crawled over to him, noticing his hands and feet were bound. She stopped short of his reach. "How'd you end up here? I thought you were in the holding center."

Billy moved his eyes toward the door. "Lucky me. I escaped." His tone was droll.

Danielle's pulse ticked up a notch. She scrambled away. "You escaped?" she asked. Alarm bells sounded in her head.

Billy pushed up on his elbow, but his bound hands sent him crashing back to the floor. "Stop your yapping and cut the tape off my hands before the crazy son of a gun gets back here."

Danielle rocked back on her heels. Her body froze with indecision. Billy's snarl when he'd threatened Ava at the fall festival flashed through her mind. She bit her lower lip, her mind reeling. Instinctively, she searched the dark room for any sign of something to free his hands. Should she?

"You threatened Ava at the fall festival."

"I wanted your boyfriend to back off. I knew the police department was gunning for me." He shook his head. "Okay, I'm not exactly a boy scout, but I'm not a killer either. And I never hurt your sister."

Pinching her lips together, she couldn't stop her teeth from chattering. "How do I know you're telling the truth?"

Billy's upper lip curled, then his expression relaxed. "You're a smart girl. If I'm the bad guy, what am I doing on this rock-hard floor of my own boat? Stop overthinking and cut the duct tape off my hands."

Danielle pushed to her feet but stayed crouched. She moved toward the opposite side of the room.

"There should be a pair of scissors in the top drawer of the desk," Billy said.

Danielle glanced over her shoulder and gave him a pointed look, but realized it was probably lost on him in the darkened room.

"I told you. This is my boat."

Danielle opened and closed three drawers before finding what she was looking for. She knelt next to Billy and worked on the duct tape on his hands. "You better hurry, speedy," he said, his voice dripping with sarcasm. She cut through the last bit of material and Billy rolled to a sitting position. He rubbed his wrists and glanced back toward the door.

"Hurry." He yanked the scissors from her hand, causing her to fall on her backside. He glared at her. A silver moonbeam reflected on the metal shears. Sucking in a breath, fear chilled her flesh. A wicked grin flashed on his face. "You are such a prima donna." He lowered the scissors to work at the reams of duct tape binding his feet. "If you want to get out of here alive, you're going to have to trust me."

"Trust you?" The expression "between a rock and a hard place" came to mind.

"For all your fancy education, you're missing the obvious."

"Which is...?" Her mind swirled. She wasn't able to focus. For all she knew, she had lost her Gram and her sister tonight.

Exhaling slowly, she willed her nerves to calm down before panic consumed her.

Billy leaned in close, his face inches from hers. Moonlight glinted in his eyes. "Parker plans to kill us both and make it look like I did it."

"Parker?" *Jimmy?* Horror squeezed her heart. "How do you...?" Her voice cracked. "Why?"

Her stomach lurched. Patrick's handsome face floated into her mind's eye. And what about sweet Ava? If Danielle died, the child would be... Danielle shook her head. She had to focus. Get out of this mess.

Billy lowered the scissors' blades to the tape. He lifted his face to stare into hers. "He obviously has something to hide. Something that you must already know." His nicotine breath whispered across her mouth. "Something he's hoping to pin on me."

Danielle shook her head. "I don't know anything." She touched her aching head. Dried blood matted her hair to her scalp in spots. "But he..." the images of tonight swirled in her head, "...he firebombed my house. He wanted to kill Jenny."

After he had failed the first time.

Patrick tapped the back of the ambulance. Jenny and Gram were safely inside. The driver took the signal and eased down the gravel driveway. Patrick had insisted they be taken to the hospital for observation. He ran a hand across the back of his gritty neck, steeling himself for whatever came next.

He turned and watched the firefighters drench the remaining hot spots. Tension twisted his gut. What if he lost Danielle too? He pushed the thought back. He refused to go there.

He paced the width of the driveway, never taking his eyes from the house. The heavy flames had been extinguished, but an acrid smoke choked the air. Black marred the white siding around every window. Two firefighters searched inside the charred house for any sign of survivors. Any sign of Danielle.

Patrick clenched his hands into fists. He could only remember one other time he'd felt this helpless. When he was stationed in Iraq and his commanding officer had told him Lisa was in a coma. A world away, there was nothing he could do.

Like now.

He paced back and forth, trying to expend some of his nervous energy. One of his fellow officers approached him. "Can't locate the chief."

"I can't deal with that now." Patrick waved the young officer away.

"We got another problem, sir." The new recruit seemed hesitant to speak up.

"Spit it out."

"Billy Farr escaped."

A cold chill ran down his spine, even as the heat from the smoldering fire coated his skin in a thin sheen of sweat. He fisted his hands and wanted to punch something. "When?"

"Sometime after dinner." The young officer wrung his hands in front of him. "We think he jammed something into the lock to prevent it from latching."

"Where was the officer on duty?" The man didn't answer. "Was it you?"

He nodded. "Chief Parker came by. Told me to take my lunch." He tipped his chin up, his jaw squared. "It was my job to make sure the cells were secure before I left."

"The chief was gone when you came back?"

"Yes, sir. It's not unusual to leave the prisoners in their cells. We have video surveillance."

Patrick's pulse roared in his head. "And you checked the video?"

The officer plowed his hand through his hair. "Yes, sir. It's missing. I tried to call Chief Parker, but I can't reach him." The officer lifted his brows. "Um, sir?"

"Spit it out." Patrick's eyes scanned the charred house, terror slicing through him. Billy Farr was out for revenge. Patrick had no time for idle chitchat.

"I'm not one for gossip, sir, but when I contacted the tech about the missing video, he told me about the messages on Jenny Carson's cell phone."

Spinning around to face the young recruit, the world seemed to move in slow motion. "What messages?"

The recruit took off his hat and scratched his head, as if regretting his decision to speak up. "The technician said he found over fifty messages on Jenny's cell phone the night she was hurt. The messages grew increasingly angry when she obviously didn't reply."

"Who were they from?" Patrick narrowed his gaze, his full attention now placed squarely on the young man.

"Jimmy Parker. I think he thought Jenny was out cheating on him."

Patrick briefly closed his eyes and let out a long breath. Had Jimmy beaten up Jenny in a jealous rage? A lump clogged his throat. Had they pursued the wrong man? A cold chill ran down his spine. Did the chief—Jimmy's father—know and cover it up?

"All clear." The firefighter's booming voice cut through his thoughts. The firefighter lifted his shoulders and let the Air-Pak slip off his back.

Patrick approached the firefighter. "No one was in the house?" His need for confirmation nearly choked him.

The firefighter took a long swig of water, then wiped his mouth with the back of his hand. "No. The house was empty."

His legs weak, Patrick lowered himself onto the bumper of the fire truck. "Are you sure?"

"We did an exhaustive search. There are no victims in the house."

A mix of relief and new fear threaded through him. Where was Danielle?

And where was Jimmy?

"You're rather chatty."

Danielle snapped her head around to find Chief Parker at the door. Her heart jackhammered against her ribcage. Parker. Chief Parker. Not Jimmy. Her head hurt too much to decipher what any of this meant.

"Now move." Chief Parker had his gun drawn. In one fluid motion, he descended on Danielle and pushed her to the side. Billy lifted his hand with the scissors.

"Drop the scissors or I'll put a bullet in your head."

"Go ahead. You're going to do it anyway." Billy's casual tone sent a chill down her spine.

Chief Parker hitched a shoulder and the corners of his mouth pulled down. "True. But I'm doing it on my terms. Now drop the scissors before I put a bullet through Miss Carson here."

The scissors dropped with a loud clatter against the wood floor. Danielle's breath came out in a rush.

Chief Parker's harsh chuckle scraped across her nerves, sending goose bumps across the back of her neck. He tipped his chin toward Danielle. "You didn't know if he'd do it, did you? You thought I was going to have to shoot you. Sometimes you just don't know who you can trust."

With the palm of his hand to her head, Patrick's boss pushed Danielle to the side. Her hand did little to soften the blow as her shoulder and then hip slammed against the wall. She glanced over her shoulder to see Chief Parker press the gun against Billy's head. "Grab the rope and tie up Danielle."

Billy clenched his jaw, seeming to weigh his options.

"Do it or I'll blow a hole through her head." Chief Parker pressed a rope into Billy's chest.

Billy shook his head and snatched the rope from Chief Parker. With a surprisingly gentle hand, Billy touched Danielle's shoulder. "Sit down."

Their eyes met and she searched his. She had to trust him. Lifting her chin, she slid down to the floor and allowed Billy to tie her hands. Then her feet. What choice did she have? Chief Parker held a gun inches from her head. Her brain struggled to reconcile the man's position of authority with his actions. She closed her eyes and thought of Patrick. And poor sweet Ava. She was hardly a mother to the child, but hadn't Ava already lost so much?

Her breaths grew shallow as Billy worked on her feet. The familiar surge of panic licked up her arms, threatening to consume her.

Talk to God. Ava's small voice popped into her head. *God is watching out for us.* Danielle drew in a shaky breath and said a silent prayer. *Dear God, I need You now. Please help me through this journey. I have trust You will deliver me to safety. I have faith.*

A long-ago verse floated through her mind—*I can do all things through God who strengthens me.* She repeated the refrain over and over.

A calmness descended upon her like a warm soft blanket. She opened her eyes and looked at Billy. He seemed to be trying to telegraph something to her with his eyes. She glanced down at her hands and realized the knot was loose. She quickly shifted her hands to hide the fact from Parker.

When Billy was done, Parker jammed his elbow into the side of Danielle's head and knocked her over. Her body crashed against the wood floor. The wind knocked out of her in a *whoosh.* She struggled to stay alert.

Parker lifted his gun and brought it down on Billy's head. The man crumbled to the floor. The crooked cop hitched a shoulder. "Would have been easier on everyone if he had stayed unconscious. Must have a hard head."

"Wait here." Parker bent over and shoved his gun into her ribcage. With bound hands and feet, Danielle wasn't going anywhere soon.

From her position on the floor, she watched as Parker set the gun down on the table. He took up position next to Billy and jammed his hands under Billy's armpits and pulled. "Man, he weighs a ton." He flicked his hard eyes toward her. "Dead weight." His lips pulled back into an ugly snarl. She stifled a gasp. Would this man's face be the last she ever saw?

A plan formulated in her mind. She had to make him talk. She couldn't just let him carry out his plan. Whatever it was, she knew it was evil. She had to slow him down. Pray help would come in time.

"Why are you doing this?"

"Because you are a royal pain. Like every other woman I've ever known." He let Billy Farr drop to the floor. His head bounced off the deck, making Danielle wince.

Parker puckered his lips. "Don't worry. He didn't feel that."

Realization began to dawn. "You were the first police officer on the scene of my sister's accident."

Silence stretched between them as she watched conflicting emotions play across his pinched features. He pulled his cell phone from his pocket and placed it on the table. "I suppose I have some time to chat." The phone vibrated. "Your boyfriend's been trying to call. Oh man..." he rolled his eyes in a huge arc, "...the women in town are going to be swooning over him."

Parker grabbed his gun from the table and pulled out a wooden chair, straddling it. "They'll think, 'Oh, how tragic. He lost his wife. Then he lost Danielle.'" A chill ran up her spine.

"I'm okay and Billy over there is okay. You haven't done anything that can't be fixed."

"Jenny's dead. And so is dear old Granny. Did you forget about the little fire back home?" He leaned over to glare into her eyes. His stale breath whispered across her cheek.

Of course she hadn't forgotten. She had been grasping at straws. Anger bubbled up, pushing back the last tendrils of fear. Survival mode.

God was on her side.

She gently tugged on the ropes binding her hands, trying not to draw attention to her movements. If given a few extra minutes, she could free her hands. Her focus shifted to her legs. Would she be able to free both her hands and feet?

She struggled to stay focused. "Why did you do this?" Her voice was remarkably calm.

Parker pinned her with a smug look. "My job is to protect."

Alison Stone

She bit back the reply that sprung to mind.

"My job is to protect my son. He's the most important thing to me. Poor kid has had one bad break after another." Parker scratched his head with the barrel of the gun. "First, his no-good mother threatened to leave me."

Cold dread drenched Danielle.

"I killed the..." He ran his hand across his mouth as if he had tasted something bitter. "I couldn't let her take my kid away from me. After everything I did for that kid—to make sure he grew into a solid man—he made one bad decision after another. Dating one bimbo after the next." He shook his head in disgust. "All women are nothing but trouble."

The rope loosened around her wrists. She wrapped her fingers around the slack bindings to secure them in place. She was too engrossed to take issue with the bimbo comment. Parker's words didn't make sense. Unless...

"You didn't beat up Jenny. Jimmy did." A major piece of the puzzle snapped into place.

Parker pushed off the chair and paced the small space. "Jimmy came to me because he'd beat Jenny unconscious. Dumb kid. Didn't know what to do." He pushed a hand through his hair. "He thought she had been out cheating on him when we were using her as a drug informant."

Parker shook his head. "Can't really blame the kid for thinking that. You know that slut let Henry sleep in your grandmother's basement sometimes. She told Jimmy it was because he had a tough home life." Parker chuckled. "Who hasn't? You can relate, right? I could have pinned this mess on him too." He hitched a shoulder. "But Billy seemed like the bigger waste of life. Get rid of him and we all win."

Parker picked up his cell and tossed it back down. "Patrick's going to send a search party for you soon." He bent

208

over Billy's body. "So I'm going to kill you and Billy. Since you and your sister ruined Billy's life, he snapped and went on a killing spree. Then, in his guilt, he killed himself. Perfect plan." He kicked the man prone at his feet. "Right down to my abducting him from jail and making it look like he escaped."

"You think Jimmy's going to let you get away with it? He loves Jenny." A shudder raced through her body, knowing full well Jimmy's love was warped. "He'll hate you forever."

"Hate's a strong word. We men have to stick together. Besides, it's a little late to worry about Jenny. The way I figure it, Jimmy will believe like the rest of them that Billy is a drug-dealing-loser turned killer. He doesn't know about anything. Naïve kid thinks Jenny really did get into a car accident. Thinks she got up after the beating he inflicted and took a drive." He shook his head in disbelief and stood up. "Stupid kid...takes after his mother. Nearly blew everything when he broke into the house to steal the phone and failed. If anyone had seen those angry texts, it wouldn't have taken long to put two and two together."

Parker grabbed Billy under the armpits again. He grunted as he dragged the lifeless body out onto the deck. Danielle drew in a deep breath and let it go, feeling time—her life—slipping away. The chief was about to kill Billy. *Then her.*

Breathing heavily from the exertion, the chief returned to her side and jammed his hands under her armpits. She shuttered her expression, refusing to give him the satisfaction of seeing her fear. But he was on a rant. "And I made darn sure Jenny stayed good and scared. Didn't want her flapping her gums, telling everyone how he beat her up. I will not let anyone ruin my boy's future."

Parker pulled Danielle out into the night air, her loosely bound feet dragging across the deck. His rough grip made her entire body ache. The wind whipped her hair, blinding her. Billy was lying near the end of the boat. One swift push and the dark waters of the lake would swallow him up. She drew in a deep breath and her body shuddered. Parker lifted her and planted her bound feet inches from Billy's head.

Parker lifted the gun to Danielle's head.

God helps those who help themselves.

She sucked in a breath and jumped.

Chapter Eighteen

Patrick raced toward the marina. Debbie Farr had called the police to report Billy's car and boat had been stolen. Sure enough, Billy's car was the only vehicle parked in the well-lit parking lot. His boat was nowhere to be found. Patrick ran out to the dock and scanned the lake. In the distance, he saw a boat bobbing. He yanked his cell phone from the clip on his belt and dialed the station, then ran to the docked police boat.

"Any word on the chief?" Patrick asked the dispatcher.

"Not yet."

"What about Jimmy."

"Found him home in his bed. Claims he has no idea where his dad is."

Patrick didn't have time to process all this. His main focus was to find Danielle. "I'm at the lake. I think I spotted Billy Farr's boat. I'm going out."

"Wait for backup. I'll have the Coast Guard out there in five minutes."

"I don't have five minutes."

Patrick jammed his phone back into its holster. He unwound the rope, tossed it aboard and boarded the vessel.

A shot pierced the night air. Icy dread surged through his veins. He jammed the key into the ignition and fired up the engine. Pushing the throttle forward, the sound of the motor and the slapping of the boat on the water's surface filled his ears.

The icy water was like a million needles assaulting Danielle's flesh. She held her breath as her body sank deeper into the murky water. She wiggled her hands, and mercifully they came free. Glancing toward the surface, she saw the wavy light seeping from the boat. Like a mermaid, she swam under the water, away from the boat. When her lungs couldn't stand it anymore, she burst through the surface and gulped in the frigid night air.

Something pinged off the water next to her head. Palms up, she pushed herself back under the surface. She lifted her legs and worked on the ropes around her ankles. The ropes—thanks to Billy—were easy to undo. Her pulse roared in her ears, but she stayed submerged. She swam under the water and reemerged a short time later. As quietly as possible, she gulped the air.

Help me, Lord. Help me.

Danielle snapped her head around at the sound of a boat's motor. It was coming right toward Billy's boat. Her heart leapt. Someone would save her. God had answered her prayers.

The sound of a second motor cut through the air. Parker was taking off in the boat with Billy still on board. The other boat was coming right toward her. She waved her hands and hollered. As if by the hand of God, the boat shifted course and came up near to where she treaded water. The motor died.

The reflective letters, *POLICE*, glowed under the moonlight. Danielle's heart soared. She kicked her legs and swam with even strokes until she reached the back of the boat. She looked up to find Patrick with an outstretched hand.

Thank You, God.

His warm hand clutched her wrist and yanked her out of the water in one fluid motion. He draped a scratchy blanket over her shoulders. "Thank God," he said, rubbing her back vigorously to get her circulation going. "I thought I'd lost you. Here, sit down."

Danielle's entire body shuddered as she sat. Patrick crouched down in front of her. She reached out and clutched his hands. "Gram? Jenny?" She struggled to form the words with her numb lips.

"They're safe." He squeezed her hands. "You're safe."

Relief swept over her. *Thank You, God.*

Huddling in the blanket, she glanced across the empty lake. "Chief Parker…" her teeth chattered "…Jimmy's dad. He's behind all this." She still couldn't believe it.

Patrick's brows drew together. "Anyone else out there?"

"Billy's on the boat. He helped me escape. You have to help him."

Patrick flipped open his cell phone and called the station. After a brief conversation, he turned to Danielle. "The Coast Guard has Chief Parker. They picked him up a few miles out. They're going to transport Billy to the hospital. He's conscious and very angry." He let out a long sigh. "It's over." He traced her tender hairline. "Let's get you some medical attention now."

"I'm fine."

"Humor me."

Patrick stood up and Danielle grabbed his hand. She pulled herself to her feet and wrapped her arms around his neck. She pressed a kiss to his lips. Warmth spread through her entire body as he encircled her waist with his strong arms. Overcome with emotion, she leaned her head on his chest. "I had faith you'd find me."

Chapter Nineteen

Danielle parked her rental car near the side door of the church's community center and popped the trunk. Three weeks had passed since Patrick had saved her from the icy waters of Lake Erie and everyone had learned the chief of police had a dark and violent past. Just thinking about it made her shudder. Pulling her coat tight around her, she walked to the back of the car. A nervous excitement fluttered in her belly. Silver clouds hung low in the sky, making her wonder if they were forecasting snow. Hardly unusual this time of year in Mayport.

She lifted the trunk lid, pushed her briefcase aside and grabbed the handles of the cardboard box filled with nonperishables. She had spent the last few weeks working fourteen-hour days trying to curry favor with her bosses. All for what?

"Danielle? Is that you?"

She spun around to find Bunny standing there, a knit cap on her head and a scarf around her neck. Winter was nearly upon them. "Good afternoon, Bunny."

Bunny flipped up the collar on her wool coat. "What a nice surprise. Is anyone expecting you?"

By anyone, Danielle wondered if she meant her son? But Danielle suspected Patrick was at work right now.

"It was a last-minute decision. I knew Ava had worked so

hard for the church food drive, and I wanted to help."

A wide smile brightened Bunny's face. "Oh, Ava's inside. She'll be ecstatic to see you."

Danielle nodded and rested the heavy box on the lip of the trunk. Her heart expanded at the thought of seeing Ava again. "I've missed her." The words flew out of her mouth before she had a chance to call them back.

"Well, I know she's quite fond of you." The older woman pressed a hand to her chest and glanced toward the door of the church's community center. "The builders have made a lot of progress on your grandmother's home."

"Yes, since the fire damage was so extensive, we decided to build a first-floor master bedroom and bath for Gram."

Bunny's eyes lit up. "And great for resale." The two women laughed. Bunny tipped her head. "I'm forever the realtor."

Momentary silence stretched between the two women before Bunny spoke again. "I'm sorry, Danielle—" Bunny twisted the gloves in her hand, "—it's hard for me to admit when I'm wrong." She reached out and took Danielle's hand.

Heat warmed Danielle's cheeks.

"I should have never judged you so harshly. I was trying to protect my son. My granddaughter." Bunny squeezed Danielle's hand, tears glistening in her eyes. "It wasn't very Christianly I'm sorry."

Danielle leaned forward and brushed a kiss across the woman's soft cheek. "I know you did it because you love your family. I understand." She herself had been doing a lot of praying and reflecting these past few weeks. Prayer had given her the strength to come here today.

Bunny's hand fluttered to her face, surreptitiously wiping away a tear. "Look at me chatting away when you have this heavy box to bring in. Can I help you?"

"I can get it, thank you."

Bunny opened her mouth to say something and then closed it again, as if thinking better of it. Danielle hiked the box up, balanced it on her hip and navigated through the doorway. She drew in a deep breath. The gym was a beehive of activity. Volunteers sorted and packed the food items.

"Here, let me take that."

Danielle's heart soared. She spun around to find Patrick standing there dressed in blue jeans and a gray T-shirt stretched across his broad chest. She lowered her eyes, finding herself blushing. He came closer, reaching for the box, his clean scent filling her nose. Their hands brushed in the exchange. "Thank you." She felt like she was going to burst out of her skin. "I didn't expect you to be here."

Patrick tipped his head. "Are you disappointed?"

Danielle smiled. Goodness knows she'd missed his handsome face. His intense green eyes. His companionship.

Before she had a chance to answer, she heard Ava yell across the gym. "Miss Danielle! Miss Danielle!" Patrick's daughter ran over and wrapped her arms around Danielle's waist and squeezed.

Her heart melted with longing. Smoothing the child's hair, she bent to press a kiss to the crown of Ava's head. "Hi, sweetheart. What a wonderful food drive."

Ava's eyes brightened. "We hope to feed over one hundred families. And you came!"

"I wouldn't miss it for the world." With the toe of her shoe, Danielle tapped the box Patrick had set down on the floor.

"I'll sort it." Ava bent over and grabbed the handle and started dragging it across the smooth gym floor toward the other boxes. She stopped suddenly and stood upright and planted her hands on her hips. "You're not going anywhere, are you?"

Danielle shook her head. "I'll be right here."

Patrick closed the distance between them and whispered in a husky voice. "For how long?" His proximity sent a tingle racing through her body.

"It depends." Danielle worked her lower lip, suddenly afraid to reveal what she had come home to say.

Reaching out, Patrick ran his warm thumb across her cheek, his minty breath whispering across her cheek. Her body quaked at his nearness. "I'm sure you talked to Jenny?"

Danielle nodded. "Thank you for putting in a good word for her. I'm relieved the District Attorney dropped all charges. I suppose he has his hands full sorting out the charges against Parker and his son Jimmy."

"I hate to even think about what happened that night." Patrick clutched her forearms. "Thank goodness Billy didn't keep a lot of gas in his boat and the Coast Guard was able to pick up him and the chief...Parker—" he quickly corrected himself, "— a mile off shore. He must have realized he'd reached the end of the road to be so compliant. We caught a break."

"Lucky for Billy too, otherwise Parker might have thrown him off the boat for spite. As it was, Billy had suffered a pretty nasty head injury." Danielle winced, remembering how Billy's head had slammed on the deck.

Patrick frowned. "Jimmy and his father were sent to Erie County Holding Center, away from Mayport. I heard they're sharing a cell for now. Jimmy doesn't have money for bail and the chief—" Patrick shook his head, "—Parker is also under investigation for the murder of Jimmy's mom. I can't imagine Jimmy's childhood. No wonder he grew up to be an abuser like

218

his father." He let out a long breath. "It's crazy how you think you know someone."

Danielle squeezed his hand. "I'm sorry. This must be hard for you."

He met her gaze. "I thank God every day that you're okay. That's what matters."

"We have a lot to be grateful for." Danielle noticed Ava unpacking the box of food and chatting with friends. "I never heard what happened to Henry."

"The DA struck a deal with him in exchange for information on his dealer. Turns out Billy provided the drugs to Henry. Billy's in some trouble, but both Henry and Jenny are lucky they can put this behind them."

"Now Jenny can go back to school. I'm so relieved she got out of her abusive relationship with Jimmy. He really had her under his thumb." Anger bubbled up just below the surface. "The only memories she has of the night of the accident are of Jimmy beating her up in a jealous rage. She remembers nothing beyond that."

"Maybe it's better that way."

Danielle shook her head in disbelief. "And the entire time his father was secretly terrorizing Jenny to keep her quiet about what happened. To protect his son. No wonder she tried to push me away. She wanted me far away from here so I'd be safe."

"It's over now." Patrick squeezed her hand.

Danielle cleared her throat, not knowing how to say what she had to say. Heat crept up her neck.

Patrick gave her a wary smile, looking a little uneasy himself. "Enough of all that. How are you?"

"Good. I—" Danielle started to say and Patrick cut her off.

"I called some police departments around Atlanta and—"

She held up her hand for fear she'd lose her nerve. An excited giggle sounded on her lips. "I quit my job in Atlanta." The words tumbled out.

His face broke into a huge smile. "Really?" His eyes widened and he took a step back.

Danielle nodded. "Really. I want to set up practice here. Help people who really need it. I went back to Atlanta and was able to save Tina's home. Now her little family won't be living on the street." She pressed a hand to her chest. "It gave me such a feeling of elation. There are a lot of people I can help here. Like Billy Farr's girlfriend. She could use some help while he sorts out his legal mess."

"I can't believe it. I thought you loved your job," he teased, stepping closer and cupping her cheeks in his hands. "What about your townhouse?"

"I'm letting Jenny live there so she can take classes at Georgia State. Get a fresh start. It's my turn to be here for Gram."

"Well, I guess now is a good time to tell you they made me police chief."

"And you were willing to give that up for me?" Her heart soared.

"I'd do anything for you," he whispered, his breath caressing her warm cheek.

"I know that...now. After I went home, I prayed a lot about the future. I want us to have another chance. Get to know one another again." She cleared her throat. "But I don't want you to feel—"

Patrick put a finger on her lips. "I know how I feel." He grabbed Danielle's hand and pulled her toward the door. "Come here. Let's talk outside."

He grabbed his coat on the way out the door. Danielle walked out ahead of him. Large white snowflakes danced in the sky. Her heart filled with joy. "Oh, I love the snow."

Patrick gently grabbed the lapels of her coat and pulled her close so that their bodies were touching. He feathered a soft kiss across her lips. "I love *you*," he whispered in a husky voice.

"I love you too." Excitement fluttered in her stomach. The words came so easily.

"Then marry me, Dani."

"What?" Overwhelmed with emotion, she bowed her head, resting her cheek on his warm chest. His heart was beating as fast as hers. She lifted her face to meet his hooded gaze. "I thought I'd move back here, set up my practice and become part of this community. Take some time."

"You are part of this community. I don't need anymore time to know what I already know. I've missed you terribly these past few weeks. I want to spend my life with you."

Joy blossomed in Danielle's heart. "Yes, I'll marry you."

A bright smile lit his face. He tucked a strand of hair behind her ear and leaned in close to press his warm lips to hers. A delightful shiver swept through her body. He wrapped his arms around her and deepened the kiss. A peacefulness filled her soul despite the winter wind whistling through the empty branches.

"Look at the snow."

They broke off the kiss in unison at the sound of Ava's delighted squeal. Heat warmed Danielle's cheeks when she noticed Ava standing in the doorway pointing to the snow.

Huge snowflakes danced and fluttered to the ground, making her dizzy in a good way. A magical way. One landed on her eyelash, making her blink. A tear—a happy tear—rolled down her cheek. Patrick kissed it away.

Some things you can never escape.

Danielle looked into Patrick's green eyes, so much like his daughter's. "I'm so happy to be home."

About the Author

Growing up, Alison Stone never imagined becoming a writer. She enjoyed math and science and ultimately earned a degree in engineering. Go Yellow Jackets!

After the birth of her second child, Alison left Corporate America for full-time motherhood. She credits an advertisement for writing children's books for sparking her interest in writing. She never did complete a children's book, but she did have success writing articles for local publications.

Finally, Alison got up the nerve to try her hand at full-length fiction. After completing a handful of manuscripts, she sold her first book to Samhain Publishing in 2011, followed a few weeks later by a second sale.

Now, Alison has the best of both worlds. From her home office in Western New York, she writes fast-paced romantic suspense while her four children are in school. It never fails to amaze her how soon the afternoon bus arrives.

Alison loves to connect with her readers. Visit her at her website, www.AlisonStone.com, or meet up with her on Twitter, @Alison_Stone, or Facebook, (AlisonStoneAuthor). Write to her at Alison@AlisonStone.com.

Romance

HORROR

www.samhainpublishing.com

CPSIA information can be obtained at www.ICGtesting.com
Printed in the USA
BVOW072325180613

323698BV00002B/34/P